T0034797

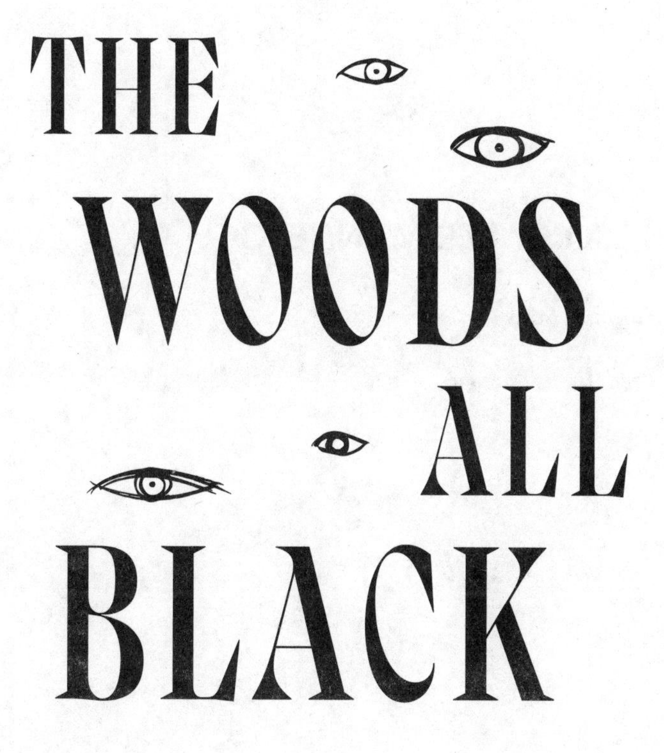
THE
WOODS
ALL
BLACK

## ALSO BY LEE MANDELO

*Summer Sons*

*Feed Them Silence*

# THE WOODS ALL BLACK

LEE MANDELO

TOR PUBLISHING GROUP
NEW YORK

This is a work of fiction. All of the characters, organizations, and events portrayed in this novella are either products of the author's imagination or are used fictitiously.

THE WOODS ALL BLACK



A Tordotcom Book
Published by Tor Publishing Group / Tom Doherty Associates
120 Broadway
New York, NY 10271

www.tor.com



The Library of Congress Cataloging-in-Publication Data is available upon request.

ISBN 978-1-250-79031-6 (hardback)
ISBN 978-1-250-79032-3 (ebook)



First Edition: 2024

Printed in the United States of America

0 9 8 7 6 5 4 3 2 1

*To all the brilliant, angry fags and dykes and gender outlaws who came before, and who taught me how to survive: this one's for you.*

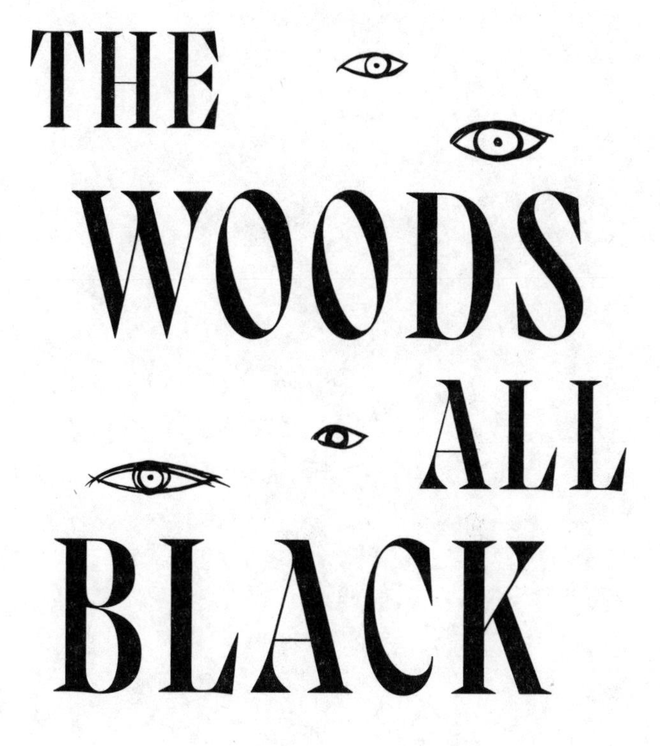
THE
WOODS
ALL
BLACK

# KENTUCKY, 1929

## 1.

The passenger train heaved to a stop at Hazard station. Coal smoke from its stacks silted the muggy air. Leslie Bruin took his cap from his knee and his travel bag from beneath his seat, tucking the former over a crop of wavy hair and the latter over a ride-sore shoulder. The train car, sleepy throughout the trek from Louisville, now bustled: girls laughing, bags thumping floorboards, the cigarette man calling out to disembarking passengers. Leslie traded a quarter for two packs as he stepped onto the platform. The end-of-summer heat hadn't cracked in the eastern counties, and a small crowd loitered in the station house shade eyeing the new arrivals. Porters offloading luggage hollered directions down-platform. With a sigh, Leslie turned toward the clamor to rescue his saddlebags.

"Miss Bruin," called a tall, sun-worn gentleman across the way.

*Miss* was far from his preferred form of address, but Leslie pasted on a smile regardless, as he recognized the speaker. "Good to meet you again, Mister Hansall."

"Jackson is fine, ma'am," he said, convivial grin creasing his face. "There's a car ready to drop us at the travel post. You need any refreshment before we hit the road?"

"I could use a sip of water, once I've collected the bags. Shall we?" Leslie gestured to the porters.

"Don't worry yourself, I'll carry those," Hansall said.

The nurses of the Frontier Service had no trouble lugging around their supplies, or else how would the work get done, but rather than kicking up a fuss Leslie smiled and nodded—amiable, businesslike. Hansall returned the sentiment with a tap to the brim of his hat and set off to make himself useful.

A squat, glittering geode propped open the station house door; the stenciled glass announced "Whites Only." South of the Ohio River those signs fruited like fungus on rotten wood. At least a quarter of the ladies whose drinks he'd stood while traipsing across Chicago on leave would be banned from stepping over the threshold—but in need of a piss and a cold drink, he crossed unimpeded. A ceiling fan stirred stale air. The solitary girl at the counter squinted at his trousers and cotton shirt then said, "Good afternoon, Nurse."

"Am I so obvious?" Leslie asked.

She rolled her eyes. "Would any other woman wear pants and boots in this weather?"

"Then I'm caught out," he said. "A soda, please?"

"Comin' right up."

As she bent to open the refrigerator the loose collar of her dress flashed silk brassiere and cleavage. Leslie stuffed his hands in his pockets, wrenching his gaze away. The clerk sat a perspiring bottle of Coca-Cola on the countertop. He swigged a mouthful of syrupy fizz and she watched silently with arms crossed under her breasts. In a city whose rules he understood, he might've chatted to her, but out here the risks outweighed the rewards considerably.

When a family came through the door with one caterwauling babe in arms, Leslie set his Coke aside. Given he'd already been read by the clerk he ducked into the ladies' restroom to do his business, emerging to find Hansall by the station entrance: hip cocked and cap beneath his arm, short sleeves cuffed nigh to the shoulder. His maleness carried such ease.

"Ready whenever," he said.

A dusty Ford awaited, its driver hanging an arm out the window. Leslie boosted himself into the truck bed beside his saddlebags. It was twenty-five miles of paved road in the Model A, then another fifteen on horseback before reaching Spar Creek—ideally ahead of nightfall. The isolated mountain town was Leslie's farthest post since rostering on with the FNS in '25, as well as his first without a partner, but Breckenridge's orders were clear. With luck Leslie would see babies birthed, children vaccinated, and adults' ailments resolved in record time; without luck, he'd be wintering in the hills.

Hansall thumped the quarter panel like a mare's flank and asked, "Mind if I ride in the cab?"

"Suit yourself, I'll rest back here," Leslie answered.

"You army girls are too tough for me." His chuckle was fond and dismissive.

The automobile creaked when Hansall clambered in. Leslie dropped his head against the wooden rail. Sunlight beat down meanly, so he dragged his cap over his face, breathing in the funk. Sweat prickled beneath his armpits and breasts. No worse than silent afternoons spent on the front by the River Marne, rotating rest shifts on the ambulance cot with a fellow nurse, their once-starched uniforms limp with the sweat of terror and exhaustion. Nothing, ever again, could possibly be so bad as the terminal months of '17 and the gore-fetid soil of Champagne—the brief season of life from which he was sometimes unsure he'd returned.

Frontier nursing might not fit his unsettled spirit, but it was the closest he'd found to meaningful labor in his decade stateside. At least delivering infants and stitching up farm accidents provided his trained hands with work while his agile, ugly brain strayed, and strained, and gnawed upon itself.

The Ford rattled out of the gravel lot, breeze nipping through the buttons of his shirt. The ride steadied as they reached the road, and as green foothills rose around them—the spurs of mountains older than time—Hazard fell away from view. Anticipating long hours on horseback, Leslie coasted into the twilight place ahead of sleep: arms crossed loose over his belly, chin drooping, leg notched over his pack. When a letter had summoned him back from leave he'd expected an assignment to the newly christened Hyden Hospital. Instead, the note informed him that the minuscule town of Spar Creek had requested a nurse—with Leslie's own name already appended by a local, Jackson Hansall, whom he'd met during a previous rotation at the coal mine another town over.

He'd been considering quitting the service to see if *this* time he could wedge himself into the role expected of him in the city: nightshift at a factory, an apartment safe enough for his girl to bring clients around, and constant vigilance against nosy neighbors ratting them out. He'd almost resolved to turn down the assignment. Then he'd come home from the bars to find another Dear John missive neatly folded on his bedside table, sealed with a mauve lipstick print and telling him what a sweet husband he'd make for some other girl, some other time. The FNS summons that arrived on its heels at least offered the comfort of orders to be followed.

The truck jounced to a halt, rousing Leslie from his stupor. He tucked his cap through his belt and mopped his face dry. A traveler's stable large enough to house twenty horses awaited them, its barn doors open wide. Manure and hay stink merged with the verdancy of the woods. Hansall rounded the backside of the truck at the same moment Leslie hopped down from the tailgate.

"If there aren't problems on the trail, we've got about five hours' ride ahead," he said.

Raspy with road dust, Leslie said, "Then let's get to it."

Bidding their driver farewell, supplying two fresh horses, and heading out along the dirt track toward Spar Creek took less time than expected. Old-growth trees rose around the trail and its hewn guide fence. Cicadas and birdsong clashed with the steady clop of hooves. Hansall led their expedition in companionable silence, his back an easy straight line used to the seat. Leslie looped his reins around the saddle knob, and the chestnut mare simply followed on. The last vestiges of his metropolitan life sloughed away as natural isolation arose.

Traversing the five-hundred-mile stretch between his northern city and a counties assignment transformed Leslie into a simpler thing, someone whose worries were limited to saddle-soreness and the pinch three centimeters beneath the shrapnel scar on his thigh—either nerve damage or a metal sliver. The nursing service patch on his jacket emptied his body of its contrary desires and replaced them with a set of tasks: no longer a person, but a purpose. Survival was simpler that way.

Light slanted through the canopy at strange low angles, and toads began to croak from the shadows. Suddenly aware of encroaching night, Leslie asked, "How much further?"

"Maybe thirty, forty-five minutes," Hansall said, unperturbed.

A brief time later they arrived at a fork in the trail and turned left. The path crested the belly of a hill then pitched downward, widening to funnel them into a protective holler. Underneath twilight stillness, water babbled over stones. Stands of oak and beech, sycamore and dense honeysuckle amplified the sound until it enfolded them. The orange sunset burned on the horizon through a break in the foliage and fireflies dazzled in the air.

Leslie kneed his mare to trot up alongside Hansall's. The gloom appointed both their faces with carnival masques of shadow. Hansall gestured ahead, his no-doubt-welcoming smile reduced to a slash of teeth.

"That'll be us through the clearing," he said.

The nape of Leslie's neck crawled. He slapped at it and his palm came away smeared with the corpse of a fat black spider. His thighs clamped, but the mare ignored him; he wiped the remains on her flank. Unease wriggled its nasty legs around inside him. Somehow, despite all his years in one form of service or another, Leslie never noticed the boundary for *too late to turn back now* until he'd already gone and crossed it.

The trail mouth spat them out right on Spar Creek's doorstep.

The town filled a bowl made by three steep, converging hills. Dual rows of clapboard buildings flanked the dirt-and-shale center lane. Farther down stood the church, homesteads with sleeping dogs on their porches, one large barn, and a schoolhouse. Beaten grass paths led into the night, ranging toward fields, animal pens, cabins and maple shacks and hunting blinds. The distant sound of workmen singing—part cow's bellow, part melodic shout—floated on the air. Leslie wheeled his horse to a stop. Light glowed behind thin curtains in all the breeze-gapped windows. One matronly woman cast them a blank glance while locking her shopfront, but otherwise the lane stayed empty. A frontier nurse's arrival usually provoked far more curiosity.

"We'll be putting you up in our back cabin," Hansall told Leslie. "Sarah should have it all readied."

"Thank you," he said.

They rode on past the general store and a smattering of homes. Near the community barn, drying tobacco scented the air. A two-horse cart with lanterns hung fore and aft bounced up the perpendicular trailhead, stacked with fresh leaves to be hung. Four men on the cusp of adulthood walked alongside. The leading pair were clearly related, both towheaded and farm-stock broad. The two lagging behind were just as clearly not: one barrel-chested and bald-shaven aside from his ginger beard, the other wiry-slight with a gathered knot of long dark hair. The youthful softness of his cheeks was offset by a flat and flinty scowl, which caught on Leslie then flinched aside. Leslie fought the urge to raise an eyebrow.

One of the blonds hollered, "Home again, Jackson?"

"Home again, and with a nurse to show for it!" he replied.

Leslie waved off their hellos—as well as their notice of his riding trousers, his army boots and cap—but Hansall didn't pause, so they cantered on away.

"Who's the kid with the attitude?" Leslie asked.

"Oh, that'd be our Stevie Mattingly," he said in a tone of tolerant amusement.

Several yards past the main thoroughfare, nestled in a copse of trees, sat a yellow-painted house with its own well, outhouse, barn, and back cabin. Hansall swung down from the rented horse and walked her across the lawn to the front post. He had built himself a comfortable life down a coal chute drawing lifeblood out of the hills, and it showed on his well-appointed land. Leslie scrubbed a thumb over his teeth, clearing grit from the ride, and hitched his mare as well. The front door opened on a woman wearing a brown skirt and white shirt belted at the waist. Her long, sandy hair hung loose.

"Sarah, meet Miss Bruin," Hansall said.

"Pleased to meet you," Sarah replied coolly.

"Would you mind showing her back to the cabin while I get the horses in?"

"Of course."

Leslie dipped a bow as Sarah descended from the porch. Bare feet and ankles flashed beneath her hemline. With his travel pack swung over one shoulder, Leslie followed her around the backside of the house. The westernmost hill swallowed the lingering sun and night spilled across the holler.

Sarah pointed him to the cabin. "There's a washbasin ready for you, and leftovers from dinner. We share the same outhouse. Knock on the back door if you're needful."

"Thank you—" Leslie began.

Sarah turned heel and strode away.

A handsome married woman giving him the cold shoulder wasn't entirely a surprise. He muttered, "Well, all right."

The single-room cabin contained an iron stove with a pipe through the roof; a brass bedframe topped by mattress, quilt, and pillow; a desk with water basin and lantern; a scuffed cedar cabinet; and a swinging pane-glass window, left open. Moths fluttered around the lantern. Lowering the latch behind him, he unfastened his boots then stripped to boxers and undershirt. Muggy night air meant mosquitoes, so with a groan he swung the window shut. He had a number of interlocking tasks he'd need to start first thing on the morrow: secure a location to run services from, determine the receptivity of the townspeople to nursing, count the children and pregnant or aiming-to-be-pregnant women, diagnose any parasitic infections or other health troubles, and ultimately establish himself as an authority . . . but never too *much* of an authority, lest the local doctors or aunties sense a threat to their monopolies.

And lastly, though the FNS would turf him if word got 'round, he had to keep an eye peeled for those secret, vital needs. Wives tired of childbearing but unfamiliar with preventatives; young men clueless on how to please their paramours; girls whose bodily education began and ended in the church pew; fellows who weren't quite fellows, and ladies who weren't quite ladies: once he'd integrated into town life, the whispers would start to arrive at his ear, and he could apply the sexological knowledge he'd gathered in Europe. He'd grown proficient at pursuing his own crosswise labors from within the troubled system he served; that was the real reason he'd stuffed himself back into a nurse's role. In the meantime, he collapsed onto the creaking mattress and drew a book from his pack. *Orlando: A Biography,* which he'd secured from a city shop during his preparations for Spar Creek. Novels had always supplied him with the comfort, understanding, and indulgence life otherwise lacked. Swaddled by fantasies of being elsewhere or else-*when,* plied with a woman's tender kisses and safe from harm—during those psychic travels he could be free, and desirable, and whole. Thumbing to his dogear, he read, *Nature, who has played so many queer tricks upon us, making us so unequally of clay and diamonds . . .*

A tree limb cracked like gunfire, too close for comfort. Leslie smacked the book closed and shot bolt upright. His reflection flickered in the window's black glass, hollow-eyed and broad-shouldered, staring reproachfully. Though he sat rigid waiting for another noise, none came, aside from the distant creek murmuring through the eaves.

# II.

The Hansall offspring, a boy around twelve and a girl no more than six, chased a flock of hens around the yard. Fistfuls of grain tossed every which way loosely qualified as feeding them. Upon spotting Leslie the girl ducked behind her brother, hands fisted in his shirt, like his reedy slouch would render her invisible. The boy's eyes were as round as bowling balls. Leslie tipped his cap and moseyed on past. Cash clip in his trouser pocket and FNS-badged jacket tossed jaunty over the shoulder, he intended to scout the main strip while waiting for Jackson to discharge his morning duties at the tobacco fields. The soap in his toiletries case had worn to slivers, and he'd spent more pack space on novels than was advisable. The general store was a good place to do some reconnaissance. A hound dog with notched ears lay snoozing on the porch, and though its eyes opened when Leslie passed, it made no effort to bark.

Sarah Hansall was hanging laundry on lines near the front of the property. Sleeves rolled to the shoulders and skirt kilted above her knees, she cut a strong figure. When she crouched to bundle damp sheets in her arms the skirts rode high enough to bare the line between tanned skin and pale on her plush thighs. Leslie cleared his throat solicitously.

Sarah dropped the sheets back into the hamper and spun. A cross pin decorated the collar of her blouse; the bridge of her nose and the apples of her cheeks glowed sun-bitten red.

"Apologies, ma'am," he said.

She planted her fists on her hips. "What is it?"

"I'm heading down to the store, could I fetch anything for you?" he offered.

"No," she replied, stone solid.

"Well, then." Leslie stalled. He weighed the merits of asking *What have I done to infuriate you so?* as sweat beaded on his nape. "Might I ask to borrow your bathing tub when I get back?"

"The children can leave it on the porch for you. Just draw from the well," Sarah said.

"Thank you."

The mistress of the house flicked a dismissive wrist. Leslie bowed as he took his leave, but she ignored his respects. The aggressive frostiness stirred his nerves—either a bad omen, or a signal of something amiss between the Hansalls. He'd completed assignments on hostile ground before, but always alongside a partner nurse. He had arrived at Spar Creek entirely alone. Only insect chirps and the constant, sloshing whisper of water accompanied him down the path from his hosts' homestead.

The road bent around the swollen foot of a hill, and on all sides rose the staggering height and heft of the Appalachians. Their immensity made the town nestled below feel paradoxically claustrophobic, as if always seconds away from being crushed. For a moment Leslie was grateful to be a lonesome thing, strolling among the earth's bones—and then the muscle aches set in. Sixteen straight hours of trains, trucks, and horses had done a number on his calves. Lucky he was the sort who enjoyed the methodical, steady, unceasing pain of a sweltering march.

Partway through the second mile of his ramble, other people began to appear: a woman with a basket looped over her elbow, a man with four fresh rabbits on a string, two children late for the schoolhouse. None of the bunch returned his greetings—and the woman even crossed to the other side of the road. Jackson had mentioned over a breakfast biscuit that the townsfolk might be nervous of outsiders, but their reception bordered on absurd. He hadn't chosen this place. The council had, at some point a few months prior, requested him *by name*. Leslie didn't care for this foreboding change, but he would offer the inhabitants of Spar Creek the respectable, steadfast nurse they'd asked for regardless.

Town proper was nigh-on deserted before noon, only some elderly men playing cards on a porch. Once folks returned from the fields and forests at suppertime, it would be busier. Leslie mounted the steps of the two-story, whitewashed general store. Speckled hens saying "Welcome!" scrawled across the front windows buoyed his spirits, until he heard the brisk conversation escaping through the screen door.

"—Sister Edwards saw them riding in last night, and she said the nurse is more mannish than Brother Hansall," a woman said.

"Well, Judy, are you really surprised?" another woman replied, nasal. "Just like Pastor Holladay's been saying, none of those city spinsters are right with God. Haven't we got enough trouble already, without government people bringing their sin on behind them?"

Unvarnished gossip carried more weight than polite introductions, so Leslie listened with care. An unattended counter with a soda fountain and one shelf with colorful paper price tags pinned beneath its canned goods stood on the other side of the door. Neither he nor the speakers could see one another.

"Sisters, come now," a man interrupted. "Recall Proverbs 20:19—the prohibition on spreading rumors. Though we should be wary of corruption, and certainly of unnatural women, we must also receive strangers in fellowship and bid them be washed in the blood of the Lamb."

Slow dread prickled. Leslie had adapted to laboring under the thumbs of preachers, demurring in public and serving women's needs in private. Spar Creek should be no different than any of a hundred other mountain settlements, each built around its church meetinghouse. However, a closely knit community whose pastor warned them daily about *unnatural* and *corruptive* influences—from the nursing service, or heaven forbid medicine itself—presented a host of problems.

What exactly had gone wrong in this town between his invitation and his arrival?

Leslie slipped on his jacket and closed the center button, darting its boxiness. The windowpane reflected an indeterminate human animal with short, greasy waves of brown hair; narrow hips and a muscular chest; a thin mouth and wide dark eyes. He ruffled the hair, drawing locks forward to soften the corners of his jaw, then grasped the brass handle of the screen door. It swung outward, squealing.

The woman who'd begun another line with "I do still think" cut herself short.

"Hullo there," Leslie called from the threshold.

The general store had been clipped from a historical catalog. Its counter ran along one wall, barring shoppers from small items like aspirin tablets, sewing needles, and other sundries tempting to slip into a pocket. Sturdy wood shelves filled the middle, with larger goods—sturdy bolts of fabric and barrels of grain, flour, sugar—closer to the rear.

"Welcome," said the woman who emerged from the back corner, hands awkwardly clasped. Her gaze stuck to Leslie's boots and trousers. "You must be the nurse Brother Hansall invited."

Curious, *Brother Hansall* rather than *the council.*

"Indeed, ma'am, I am her. Miss Leslie Bruin, originally from Illinois, though I've spent the last several years traveling around

Kentucky." He pasted on a smile for the clerk as well as the younger lady and middle-aged man behind her, as if he hadn't overheard a damn thing. "Who might you all be?"

"Judy Ellis," the clerk answered.

"Sally Greenfeld," said her companion, whose face had gone mottled pink.

"Ames Holladay, councilman and pastor," the man said. His eyes were slate blue, his cropped hair and beard chestnut brown threaded with silver. Leslie accepted a dry press of his knuckles. The flint of their appraisals slid cross-purposes, sparking. "On behalf of the Church of God, I bid you welcome."

"I'm glad to be welcomed. I found myself in need of a few staples, and thought I'd introduce myself around town in the process," he said with a nod to the shop.

"Yes, of course," Judy said. Butter wouldn't melt in her mouth.

Leslie laid his performance on thick: "Being able to meet new people is the best part of this job, I reckon. I've been five years with the service, but lending assistance to mothers and babies never gets any less fulfilling."

Sally ducked her chin, suitably abashed, but Judy and the pastor stood firm—either assuming their voices hadn't carried, or entirely unbothered by the prospect.

"Our people believe motherhood is a gift of God, far more than it is a matter of medicine or science," Holladay said, prayerful-quiet voice belying an inflexible coldness.

"I personally assure you, the FNS does not disagree," Leslie said. "Whatever you might've heard, our founder Missus Breckenridge is a staunch maternalist—"

"Excuse me, but I'm afraid I was on my way to attend a congregant," the preacher interrupted. Judy tittered, nervous. "If you wish to speak with me about your purposes in Spar Creek, please attend the sermon tomorrow. I'd appreciate seeing you in the pews."

Despite saying he'd be taking his leave, Holladay waited for a response—or for deference.

"Thank you, sir, I will," Leslie conceded, affecting a subordinate to his CO.

The pastor nodded, pressed the women's shoulders in farewell, and exited. Message delivered and received: *You are not in charge here.* The clerk and her friend looked at one another, the ceiling, the windows, anywhere but his direction. Leslie marinated briefly in the awkwardness, before clearing his throat and asking, "Could I get some soap?"

After his first sortie into town, Leslie beat a strategic retreat to the Hansall house. Unpacking supplies from his saddlebags was thankfully meditative. Arranging rubber aprons and gloves, soaps and medications, syringes and scalpels and stitching needles, allowed Leslie time to settle his growing nerves. The final items were a pair of padded leather cases containing glass vials. Pertussis, smallpox, and typhoid had all become preventable by vaccination nearly within his lifetime. Leslie lifted each individual vial to the light, ensuring no cracks from transit. Only a single sterile seal had ruptured; he discarded the damaged vial, then nestled the rest back into their cases to be stored in the bureau.

The pastor worried him as much as the silent treatment he seemed to be receiving from residents. Even before the Western front—and further still before dissolute peacetime years in Paris, smoking marijuana cigarettes over Hirschfeld's publications and trawling clubs where the femmes wore no knickers—he'd done a bad job at girlish camouflage. As an unrepentant invert thirty years of age, the skill was now entirely gone, and with each post ingratiating himself to an audience of suspicious locals began all over again. However, wander far enough out into the hills and no one could begin to imagine their nurse was a queer. Instead, they saw an unmarriageable failure aiming to spend "her" tenderness on someone else's babies. Misrecognition protected him better than lackluster costuming, and so long as he threaded the pinhole of respectability, he stayed safe enough.

Something about Spar Creek already felt crooked, though, itchy as an armpit mosquito bite. At least Jackson had promised to introduce him to an older auntie later that afternoon, someone who'd be guaranteed to know folks' business.

By the time he'd bathed in cool water, gotten presentable again, and hung his scrubbed clothes over the porch rail to dry, Hansall returned on horseback. The man's shirt was unbuttoned to the middle of his belly and his thicket of chest hair glistened. Flecks of tobacco leaf clung to his sunburnt arms and coal-stained hands. Leslie longed briefly for harvest labor among the men, rather than the uphill climb of socializing laid before him.

"Give me a minute to wash up, and we'll see Marge before supper," Hansall hollered across the yard.

Leslie puffed through two precious Marlboros waiting. Once his scrubbed-pink host returned, Leslie collected his borrowed mare from the barn and the pair set off. A smattering of paths carved out of the forest presumably led to other homesteads—and farther in the distance, the tree line consumed the road entirely. Jackson clucked at his horse and turned toward a thin trail. The forest swallowed them up, and abruptly, the creek's regular murmur intensified to a low roar. Leslie's arm hair stood on end. Within the last twenty-four hours he'd almost gotten used to the background noise, but once magnified it was like a radio dial tuned to static. The mare whinnied fretfully.

"Creek runs right behind Auntie Marge's house," Jackson said over his shoulder.

"Sure does sound like it," he replied.

The woods gave onto a lot dotted with stout dead stumps. Like sentries, the first two had been decorated with blue glass bottles strung on knotted cord. A shotgun house rested near the far edge of the clearing. A woman in her late sixties sat on the porch in her rocking chair: iron-grey hair and life-spotted cheeks, a solid body that filled out the seams of her housedress. At her feet, two orange cats lounged.

"Be welcome," she greeted.

Jackson dismounted and said, "Aunt Marge, this is Miss Leslie Bruin from the nursing service."

"Thank you for agreeing to chat with me," Leslie added.

While Jackson tied their horses to graze, he and the older woman appraised each other. Jackson had described the auntie as someone who put a high value on her solitude, practiced a studied neutrality in town affairs, and yet somehow seemed to know the details of everyone's private matters. From prior experience, Leslie understood the need to tread carefully lest he nudge her off the fence in the wrong direction.

"Would you care for some coffee?" Marge offered.

"Yes, ma'am," Leslie said.

Marge gestured to the bench opposite her rocker and went back inside. Leslie sat, as did Jackson. Marge emerged a moment later carrying two mugs of lukewarm coffee skimmed on top with a splash of cream.

"You'd like to know about Spar Creek," she said.

"Whatever you might be able to share," Leslie said. "I had an odd encounter with some folks and the—uh, preacher at the store earlier. Made me curious whether some trouble has been brewing, since the council sent 'round for me?"

"Pastor Holladay means well, I'm sure," Jackson interjected.

The sour-lemon pinch of the auntie's mouth implied she thought otherwise, but all she said was "I'm an old woman, Nurse, and try to stay out of whatever trouble folks cook up for themselves down about town. But the pastor's sermons are singed around the bottom with hellfire, you'll find."

"Well, how much sway does his scriptural interpretation hold?" Leslie asked.

The rocker treaded back and forth, creaking, while the auntie considered him. She seemed to be peeling away his layers, from uniform down to flesh and bone; the stillness that settled over him on being *seen* was preylike. A crow's caw burst from the roof above them, herald or psychopomp. He couldn't tell whether the truths she read from him raised her estimation, or lowered it.

"I will tell you," Marge said carefully, "that there are strange currents running under Spar Creek, and a preacher who sets himself foremost against devils has good reasons to find them wherever he is able."

# III.

The family Hansall, done up in respectable dress from youngest child to patriarch, left together for Saturday service, with Leslie trotting along at their heels. He'd chosen to wear his usual trousers, boots, and FNS jacket. Their party merged with a steady trickle of others; conversation ebbed and flowed between families, trading details about the harvest, a new fabric at the general store, a lamed horse. Clusters formed, but nobody attempted to match pace with the Hansalls for the sake of chatter. Instead a filmy bubble of silence enclosed them.

Judging by the surreptitious glances, Leslie's presence on the walk to church had come as a surprise. In how many sermons before his arrival had the preacher insinuated that the coming nurse would be a heathenish type, he wondered. While it was true that he'd rather muck a stall with his bare hands than enter a house of god, strategic maneuvers to assimilate were another matter.

The church's white spire pierced a cloudless, bluejay-bright sky. Beside the double doors, Pastor Holladay stood surveying the courtyard and greeting his flock as they entered. His gaze caught on the Hansalls, and Leslie marked the shift in his expression from benevolent approval to frowning coolness around the moment he noticed the trousers. With Jackson leading, Sarah and the children in the middle, and Leslie bringing up the rear, they marched on through the doors.

When Holladay clasped Leslie's hand, he said quietly, "While I'm joyous to see you in attendance, for future sermons I must request proper attire."

"Apologies, sir," he said. "The services back home aren't particular so long as all congregants are covered above the knee."

Holladay squeezed his hand so hard the knucklebones ground together. Discomfort verging over onto pain lit through his wrist. Leslie's smile went stiff, and the preacher said, "Now you have been made aware. As a matter of respect, please seat yourself in the final pews today."

The impulse to jerk free had barely registered by the time Holladay released him. Fingers tingling with punishment unseen by the line of folks behind him, he escaped the vestibule and collapsed onto an empty back bench. Seated farther ahead, Jackson flung an arm over his pew, searching until he spied Leslie. He tipped his chin but Leslie gestured a refusal. The ten o'clock bell clanged as the people of Spar Creek filtered inside. The church building held at least 150 bodies; as of last census, the town had numbered barely less than 175. There were at least fifteen children in attendance, and plenty of women of childbearing age, either with their parents or on a husband's arm.

In keeping with Leslie's past experiences in the eastern counties, every single face in the crowd from oldest granny to youngest babe was white. Breckenridge's nursing service forwarded her personal politics, and thereby his posting at Spar Creek was surely related to its racial demographics. Familiar, complicit discomfort wriggled in his belly.

Another person slid onto the end of Leslie's pew, dressed in a grey blouse and plain burgundy skirt. Road dust coated the dragging hemline and workman's boots peeked from underneath. The doors swung shut with a thunderous clap, Holladay projecting country competence as he strode past them to the pulpit. A curtain of black hair swung forward as the newcomer bent to grab the hymnal, obscuring her face; her knuckles were rough, stained green in the cracks. On the watch for misfits, Leslie perked like a spaniel—and then the girl cast him a sour glance. Even outside the tobacco fields, without the context of trousers and male company, the crooked nose bridge and flat mouth were unmistakable. The young man Hansall had called Stevie Mattingly sat alongside him on the penitents' bench, wearing what must be considered appropriate dress for the pastor's sermon.

Conflicting impulses arose: pretend he hadn't recognized Mattingly and wasn't aware of the possible humiliation, or acknowledge a kindred spirit. Before he could organize his thoughts, Holladay intoned from the front, "Please be seated, and let us begin."

The handsome fellow slouched, songbook propped laxly on crossed knees. As the congregation lifted their voices in song, neither—*he?*—nor Leslie joined.

"Yes, praise the Lord," Holladay cried over the fading chorus. His booming voice rang from the rafters and reverberated in Leslie's skull. Murmuration rose from the congregational body, breathing as one. "He has given me a sermon for you, today, a sermon to stand as a bulwark against temptation. We are surrounded, we, the foot soldiers of righteousness. We are *beset* on all sides, and we must hold back the tide of sin before it washes our people under."

"Yes, brother," a man responded.

"You see, the devil works on good Christians not only through temptation but through confusion." Holladay swung his arms wide, offering a paternal embrace. Leslie gnawed the tip of his tongue. "Worldly people may tell you to dismiss your natural fulfillments, but as the book of Genesis tells us: 'So God created man in his own image, in the image of God created he him; male and female created he them.' *Male and female created he them.* And I have seen, you know I have seen, those sinners who reject their roles; they are as children, unguided, feasting until they are sick—feasting upon fleshly desires. Their souls cry out for repentance but they do not heed the call!"

An approving rumble rose on all sides, bounced back growling from the ceiling. On the other end of the pew Stevie fidgeted, uncrossing legs and digging heels into the floorboards. Holladay cast a theatrical gaze across the room, a carnival barker's impression of eye contact. He thumbed open the pulpit Bible and tipped his chin.

"I preach today on our separate spheres—on propriety, and chastity, and modesty. Because you know that if any door is left open for the devil to slither through, our spiritual home will be lost; only faith keeps he and his minions at bay. And so we begin at Deuteronomy 22:5—'The woman shall not wear that which pertaineth unto a man, neither shall a man put on a woman's garment: for all that do so are abomination unto the Lord thy God.'"

The faint buzz in Leslie's blood grew to an anxious roar. Though no heads angled their way, he felt the pressure of eyes upon him and his rigid young compatriot. The meat of his body remembered being penned as a place turned nasty, be it bar, foxhole, or ambulance. Fleeing the room would serve no purpose—he was attending the sermon to demonstrate how *normal* he could be—but he'd grown to expect a fist to back of the head shortly after being called *abomination*.

"Women are holy," the pastor continued. "But in their innocence they are weak-willed, and this weakness leads them astray. They must submit to firm guidance from their fathers, their husbands, their community, and ultimately their Lord."

With economical, clipped motions Stevie set the hymnal aside, stood ramrod-straight, and walked out of the building. Holladay paused at the swish and slam of the doors, then smacked the pulpit to break the resultant hush.

"You see, our girls are unruly! And it is our responsibility to discipline them, rather than allowing them to fraternize and debase themselves—resist our caring hand though they surely will." Fire on his face, the preacher man pointed right at Leslie. Breath hung in his chest. "What may pass in the sinner's world, does not pass in the godly world. First Timothy 2:12, 'But I suffer not a woman to teach, nor to usurp authority over the man, but to be in silence.'"

Wailing babble sprung from the front pew as an elderly matron tossed herself to the ground, arms and legs spasming. Holladay knelt beside her at once to press his hand onto her forehead. The other he lifted heavenward, a lightning rod for the divine. Tongues flowered cacophonously as other congregants joined the confusion with their ecstasies, and Leslie slipped from the oppressive sanctuary. Crisp, breezy heat and sunlight knocked his frantic brain down into his body again. The contrast between outside and inside was stark.

Leslie trotted down the porch stairs and around the side of the building, only to happen abruptly upon his fellow escapee. Leaned against the fence with the top buttons of his blouse undone, boot heel propped to lift one knee and skirt tucked between his legs to mimic pants, Stevie stood transformed. A lit cigarette dangled from his mouth. His attention flicked onto Leslie and away, performed indifference. Smoke haloed his head in wisps.

"May I join you?" Leslie asked.

The youth gestured to the spot beside him.

These dance steps Leslie knew by heart. On approach, he drew the Marlboros from his chest pocket, then posted up against the rail two inches closer than arm's length and angled in Stevie's direction. The cigarette paper between his lips comforted him as he patted his pockets for a matchbook.

"No need," said Stevie in a husky drawl.

He proffered a brass flick-lighter, thumb already working flint. The flame rose hot and ready. Leslie leaned forward with the tip of his cig, cautiously looking up past Stevie's hand from beneath his lashes. Under direct sunlight the blouse revealed a distinct lack of corsetry, silhouetting a swell of breast and pebbled nipple. One long draw caught the spark and filled his mouth and throat with silken heat. He cast his gaze back out along the fields. Stevie watched him sidelong, though Leslie couldn't guess the balance of curiosity and aggression in his weighted stare.

Leslie exhaled, then said, "An experience, that was."

In response he received an aggrieved snort.

"The name is Leslie Bruin, if you hadn't already heard," he offered.

The youth said, "Stevie Mattingly."

Quiet settled as each smoked through their respective cigarette. With the church still so close, Holladay's sermon echoed faintly through the walls. Leslie fought off a shudder. Auntie Marge had said there were six unmarried, eligible girls in Spar Creek, and he found himself curious whether she'd counted Stevie.

"May I ask how old you are?" he ventured.

"Eighteen," Stevie said. Leslie opened his mouth to inquire further, but the boy scuffed his cigarette on the fencepost and cut him short with, "It's none of my business, but if you'll listen to some advice: get out of here. Fast as you can."

Stevie shoved off the fence rail, skirt collapsing around his boots, and strode away with nothing more than a flick of the fingers. Leslie fumbled his cigarette in his haste to stand, calling, "Wait!"

Stevie ignored him, and a crash of muffled applause signaled the sermon's end.

At the lip of the Hansall homestead, following an interminable walk where all pretended nothing strange had occurred, Jackson caught his elbow and said, "Go on out back to the creek if you need to settle."

On the lee side of the cabin, creepers obscured a footpath leading into the woods. Leslie discarded his jacket and tucked *Orlando* under his arm. The trail barely accommodated his shoulders; untrimmed branches drooped under their own weight, glossy fat leaves tickling the tips of his ears. The ever-present sound of water increased by degrees from low whisper to conversational babble. His synapses still pulsed with the premonition of threat. The crash would come later, as it always did with shellshock, but for the moment he remained afire. A garter snake whipped its body across the path; under the canopy the air was green, wet, and rotten. Shale outcroppings and polished rocks littered the dirt with increased frequency until the thinning trees gave ground onto water. The creek poured clear down a broad, shallow bed—but what stole Leslie's breath were the glittering mineral stones scattered across its banks, beneath its current. An unearthly rainbow refracted through fragments of fluorspar, their pinks and greens and milky violets trapped behind the water's liquid glass.

Leslie's boots crunched over slivers ready to lay open flesh as he crouched to dip his hand. The creek was six or eight inches at its deepest. The current tugged firmly toward town, far stronger than anticipated. The forest's majesty pressed upon his shoulders.

Silty rich soil thrummed with age that belied the name *Spar Creek,* marking the brief and stolen history of its ownership. A peculiar hush descended; beneath the babble of the creek he heard something *else.* Strain though he might, the counterpoint remained faint, a disconcerting whisper at the limits of his ear. The rippling stream disrupted his reflection, cast strange black hollows across his eyes and parted lips. Shadows spread across the squared lines of his jaw, the plane of his forehead. The glassy surface rose toward him.

A crow's call brayed through the stillness.

Leslie startled, the hypnotic draw broken. The water showed him nothing more remarkable than his own exhausted face. It had been some long while since he'd experienced a vivid hallucination. After armistice, during his first months away from the carnage at the Marne, he'd been struck often and powerfully by recollections of what he'd seen and sensed there—or, as he always corrected himself, what he *believed* he'd seen and sensed. Those visions were no more than desperate, frightful dreams dredged up by a mind sheltering itself from horrors too great to bear. Here, too, the forest was merely a forest; Spar Creek was merely a creek, though a striking one.

Lingering tightness between his ribs disagreed. Leslie flicked his fingers in the water to disrupt his reflection and settled on his heels. On the far side of the water the walking path carried on. Mildly overgrown underbrush aside, the trail seemed to see regular enough use. Softened ground near the bank even held footprints, as if someone else had passed through recently. The path, he assumed, was a deer track. Hansall would be a fool if he hadn't set game traps on his property, or even beyond where it ended and unclaimed forest began.

Nothing about the footprints themselves was remarkable. Yet an immaterial pressure coasted along the nape of his neck, the sort of preternatural awareness he had tried to abandon at the front. Someone, or some*thing*, had laid its attention on him. That much his body knew. The forest paused. Even the cicadas ceased their greedy rattling, leaving only the mumble of the Spar rising to the sky. Leslie pressed his hand onto the creek bed, intending to boost himself upright—then startled at sharpness cleaving into his flesh. Pink water soaked his shirt cuff as he lifted the wound overhead. Sunlight caught on a glassy shard of mineral lodged in his palm. On the opposite bank, distant enough to remain unseen but close enough to hear, a presence rustled through the trees.

Leslie hastened backward, watching the empty trailhead until the woods closed around him. Under the canopy he turned tail to run. Deer, coyote, or man: whatever moved through the ground cover, he had no desire to confront it bloodied and unarmed.

# IV.

By the close of the seventh day in Spar Creek, nothing at all had happened. Leslie had never before in his life experienced the thorough efficiency of his ostracization from the town. None of the tasks he'd set himself were completed, or truly even begun; each morning he set out fresh, and each afternoon he returned stymied to sit on the cabin steps with his hands clasped between his knees. He'd been granted no base of operations, but neither had he any operations to *perform*. On the first day the schoolmistress rebuffed him, firmly stating that the parents of Spar Creek had forbidden him from speaking to the children. On the second, third, and fourth days he'd gone door to door, methodically calling at every household—and, to the last, had either been left standing on porches while residents inside ignored him or turned away like an unwelcome salesman by the folks with manners.

On the fifth day he rested. By night he'd been smothered in his sleep with memories of bones churned loose from trench mud, dragged beneath the cold clinging muck; when he rose from his bed to light the lanterns, his ears itched with ghostly whispers. The eerie combination of isolation and entrapment, the watchful eyes that skittered away if he turned to catch them, had frayed his nerves to shreds. On the sixth and seventh days his rounds remained brief: he delivered polite introduction cards to local businesses and farm posts, pressing them into palms that stayed dead-fish limp. Leslie couldn't bring himself to read his novels, or to wander the woods; even those idle pleasures he was denied by ratcheting tension that built, and built, and built.

At last, once Sarah and the children had disappeared into the kitchen following another tense shared supper, Leslie rapped his knuckles on the table and said to Hansall, "What on earth is going on in this town, sir?"

The man had the grace to look abashed. "I gather you've had trouble."

"You sure could say so," Leslie replied. "All these folks treat me like a pariah, and I'm at the end of my wits. What am I doing here?"

"Honest, when the council voted to send 'round for a nurse, folks were agreeable enough. But with the tobacco harvest come due, and the pastor's business with the Mattinglys—maybe it's a bad time, bad timing," he finished limply.

"I see," he said.

Leslie kept to himself the suspicion that no time would be a *good* time for the FNS to come to Spar Creek, but there might be some truth beneath Jackson's words. Harvest meant all hands on deck, doubly so for a town that depended on a single cash crop like tobacco. Even before the Great War culled a generation's men, tomboyish sorts would be permitted to assist in field labor, with the unspoken assumption that they'd return to their usual roles after the harvest. Perhaps Mattingly had made the mistake of assuming he'd be compensated and respected as an equal by the men he worked alongside. Maybe he had maintained his masculine dress past the acceptable excuse of temporary labor. Leslie had seen similar dramas play out before, in life and in stories. An ongoing dispute such as that would cast his workmanly, trousered presence in an even harsher light: at best an unwanted complication, at worst a corruptive influence.

Hansall licked his lips, glancing at the kitchen door, then leaned closer. "Tell you what, the next council meeting is tomorrow night. I'm heading over to the mines in the morning, won't be back in time to attend, but if I can rustle you an invitation through Tim Landsdale, would you go make your case with 'em?"

Leslie nodded shortly. "Much obliged."

"I'll get after him tonight," he said.

Sarah nudged the door open and raised her brows at them. "Will I have to sweep around your feet?"

"Sorry, ma'am," Leslie said. "Thanks for supper."

Leslie saw himself back to the cabin. Regardless of the outcome, his first week's report would be due. Hansall had offered to carry his mail with the outgoing stack in the morning. He'd set his forwarding address from Chicago to a PO box in the mining town across the eastern hills, the closest location within postal service. He entertained a brief fantasy of receiving a love note from any of his city girls, but he'd built no strong intimacies with any of them. Only the passing of Leslie's mother and the settlement of her meager estate had pulled him back to the States from Paris; he had few ties anywhere, and fewer still whom he might consider close. Cast out from Spar Creek's social circles as well, the pin sting of loneliness grew.

The oil lamp at his elbow cast an unsteady glow. A larger lantern borrowed from the barn hung from the rafters, its flicker chasing black shadows into the corners. Leslie had draped a curtain across the window. Sleeping with the night staring straight onto his bed gave him the willies.

Leslie addressed his first letter to his supervisory officer, Nance Jefferson, then continued:

*Mister Jackson Hansall has been a circumspect and friendly host, but without fail, the people of Spar Creek are highly resistant to the assistance of a nurse. It feels as if we were never invited to begin with. Aside from the Hansalls, I have been unable to secure rapport with any single person; the pastor publicly disapproves of working women, and also educated women, which is certainly a contributing factor. While I intend to continue my efforts, perhaps at least far enough to provide vaccinations, my hopes for providing services around midwifery and mothering have begun to disperse. I do not anticipate a change in popular attitudes within the following weeks and await your instruction regarding the point at which discontinuing the post would be allowable. Nevertheless, the demographic report is as follows, drawn from field observation . . .*

Throughout the rest of the letter Leslie gestured toward the mitigating circumstances—*I have the sense there are larger secrets regarding the people of Spar Creek which I do not know and cannot begin to guess*—while avoiding particulars his managers would find untoward, such as the presence of Stevie Mattingly. He also elided the happenings at the creek and his unsettled dreams, for which there was no scientific explanation. Better not to inform one's supervisors that a nasty sermon had brought on a mild shellshock relapse.

He hadn't returned to the solitary footpath, but the jagged fragment of fluorspar he kept on the desktop. He rolled the thirsty edge under his index finger to see the light crawl through its milky lens. Official correspondence completed, he began a second letter addressed to Addie, his dearest fellow invert up North. Forty-seven years old, wifed to a pretty girl, built like a tank, owner of a club: an aspirational friend. In the opening paragraphs he bemoaned Spar Creek's rancidness from the mosquitoes to the preacher man to the failing job, before casually noting: *Met to my surprise a rather gay young thing, who seems to smoke cigarettes as often as us.* If the message were intercepted, nothing had been revealed, but Addie would understand. *What to do? I'd rather get up and go than stay here another minute.* He signed off, *Exhaustedly yours, Les.*

A third crisp white page awaited. Hansall might get him a chat with the council, but on his own he had no power to loosen the town's resistance; it was by the skin of his teeth that Jackson convinced his wife to host Leslie at their dining table. The single avenue he hadn't pursued was Pastor Holladay himself... and though he'd rather eat sand, he'd run dry on options. How far could Leslie stretch his compliance, his performance of respectability, to draw an ounce of trust from someone set against him? Nib met paper, withdrew—met paper and withdrew again. He could endure further frights and humiliations, or he could simply abandon his post. Perhaps this rejection by Spar Creek was the sign he'd been waiting for to end four years with the FNS spent stumbling after the usefulness and camaraderie he'd experienced on the front—but remaining as unfree as ever.

Trouble was, he didn't care for the thought of letting Ames Holladay *win.*

By the time his bladder pinched, nothing further had been accomplished besides ruining the page with wasted ink. Leslie took up the lantern and stepped into his unlaced boots, then hesitated on the porch. The outhouse was less than twenty feet away, but night in the hills had physical density. Whatever moonbeams drifted down to the tree-clogged bowl of the valley were unable to penetrate the blackness coating the homestead. The glow of an upper window in the main house, like a low-hung star, failed to touch the ground below.

Though he was generally unflappable, the thought of descending into the dark yard made Leslie feel as if his boots had fused to the porch. He was no stranger to night-blind fields. On the front he had crept through them on his elbows and belly, festering mud between his fingers, following the animal cries of injured men. As a frontier nurse he had forded icy rivers guided by nothing but a lamp, the North Star, and determination. But something about Spar Creek twisted at the back of his mind, as it had from the first: a subtle *wrongness* deeper flowing than the bad intentions of one pastor and his congregation. The babble of the distant waterway slithered against his eardrums.

Leslie heaved one long sigh from the depths of his belly, recalling how much worse he'd survived than going for a piss in the woods. Shame propelled him down the stairs and across the yard, where he relieved himself with the outhouse door wide open, buttoning his trousers one-handed with lantern held aloft. Crossing the yard once more required as much psychic effort; exposure crawled along the hairs of his forearms as he crept through the grass.

He was no more than halfway to his goal when crashing, clumsy-quick motion from behind the trees shattered the quiet. Leslie's stomach lurched; it was as if his nerves had been a summons. The safe harbor of the cabin was far from reach. He spun and brandished the lantern, switchblade palmed. Its flick-clasp releasing accelerated the thumping of his heart. He'd used that knife before, and he'd do it again if needed. From the trailhead a man-shaped shadow emerged, one patch of darkness separating from the other.

Voice crisp and steady, Leslie commanded, "Hold there, friend."

"Fuck," spat the intruder—slurred by liquor, or a swollen mouth.

"Slowly, into the light." Switchblade laid against his thigh, he edged nearer. "What are you doing out here?"

"None of your business," the person hissed.

Leslie shuffled forward one more step.

The lantern cast its meager glow across Stevie Mattingly, glossed his purpled lip and the fresh blood that streamed from his nose, down his chin, onto a bared collarbone. He clutched a ragged, torn shirt closed over his chest. Bitter sweat and alcohol stink wafted from him; leaf litter was tangled into his unbound hair. Livid, toothy bruises speckled the meat of his neck and shoulder. Leslie's body snipped away fright to make room for battlefield practicality. As both a nurse and a soldier, he'd encountered this scene before—and surely would again, given the world's nature. Leslie closed and pocketed his switchblade.

"Easy, easy there," he said.

Stevie bared red-stained teeth. "Move," he said.

"Let me help you." Leslie stood still, hands lifted, and tried to secure eye contact. Settling himself would settle his patient. He said, "I'm trained at doctoring, remember?"

The boy-creature spat a wretched mouthful of phlegm at his feet. Despite the shaking of his legs, he made to walk around Leslie. With no intention of contact, Leslie lifted a hand across his path and tried again: "Please, I understand, but you'll need—"

Stevie knocked his arm aside hard enough for the elbow joint to pop. Calmer than Leslie expected, though without turning to face him head-on, he said, "If you lay a hand on me I will beat you within an inch of your fucking life."

"Take this, at least." Leslie proffered the lantern, hook dangling over his first three fingers. Stevie hesitated. Past the bubble of its glow lay only blackness. "I won't tell a soul. I swear to you."

Whether from drink or pain or the combination, Stevie's reach was loose-fingered. For a moment he grasped Leslie's hand together with the hook. Their eyes finally met, accidental and instinctive; Leslie could not marshal his own expression, and Stevie flinched like a spooked horse. The lantern swayed madly, skeleton shadows dancing over his jaw and cheekbones. He jerked the light from Leslie's grip with a grimace and turned toward home. The sway of his steps meandered, and Leslie stood watching the will-o'-the-wisp light bob into the distance until it disappeared. He had been angling himself toward quitting his assignment, he realized in hindsight, but what he had seen emerge from the woods realigned his priorities. If those were the sorts of dangers flowing beneath the surface of Spar Creek, perhaps his service had some use after all, a reason to continue fighting.

The homestead's upstairs light snuffed out. Leslie swallowed a coppery mouthful of fear-spit. Solitude rarely felt so threatening. Each time he closed his eyes after climbing in bed, feet tangled in the quilt, his body remembered how it had felt years before when a man's hand had clamped over his own mouth: his teeth had punctured the meat of his cheek, blood viscous on his tongue with nowhere to go but down his throat. He rose from the mattress to check the door latch, over and over again, and peered from the covered window out into the wall of trees.

# V.

Leslie trudged across town, satchel bouncing on his hip, keenly aware that Hansall—perhaps his one defense—had ridden out that morning without him. In the man's absence, the pressurized confines of Spar Creek cinched another notch tighter around his neck. He understood the plan he'd laid for himself was scouting behind enemy lines: a significant risk with a narrow margin for success. But if the council invitation arrived as intended, he might benefit from laying groundwork—and doing some reconnaissance.

His wrinkled skirt swished through road dust. Losing the trousers bothered him, but given the humid summer afternoon, the draped cloth allowed a welcome breeze on his nether regions. On the map he'd sketched across seven days of inefficient wandering, the church and parsonage were marked with splotchy crosses. The spire cast a knifing shadow across the road. He unlatched the parsonage gate, which faced onto the house's slope-roofed mudroom backside. Snatches of an ongoing conversation floated around from the front porch, and Leslie softened his footfalls on the cushioning bluegrass. It wasn't the sort of information gathering he'd planned on doing, but he wasn't about to waste an opportunity.

"Delia Mattingly called Ames over for a prayer visit this morning," one woman, presumably the preacher's wife, said. "She told him it was terribly urgent, and he mustn't delay."

"Surely for that child of hers," the other responded.

Leslie held his breath. If anyone happened across him loitering by the parsonage, he hadn't a single excuse—but given how townsfolk already treated him, their opinions couldn't be worsened much.

"Whoever else? She was moaning on at sewing circle about how Stephanie wouldn't budge on the Marshall boy's proposal last month, no matter how she scolded. Delia has no rule over that child."

A betrothal refused *last month*—perhaps just after the council sent for the FNS.

"Hardly a surprise without a father in the house, Jesus rest his soul. She needs to get that girl married off, and the whole town knows Stephanie shouldn't be putting on choosy airs, carrying on with those men every day how she does." An ugly scoff. "Unheard of, before the war. That willfulness wouldn't have withstood a good strapping or two."

As he listened on, Leslie's gut sank. His lantern might've seen young Stevie home safe, but by first light his wounds would tell their own stories, and he could guess how poorly these people would respond. Holladay had been with the Mattinglys for hours and hours already.

"Best pray for Ames's successful intercession, then," the other woman said.

"Amen."

Chair legs dragging across boards. Leslie leapt into motion as well, managing a few steps forward before the preacher's wife leaned over the porch rail to dump pea shells onto the compost. When she lifted her head and spotted Leslie she jumped, dropping the basket.

"You know, I also heard—" her friend began.

"My, you startled me!" she barked.

The friend shut up quick.

"Apologies, ma'am," Leslie said. He handed the bushel basket over the rail. "I came to drop a calling card for your husband, at the suggestion of Mister Hansall and his wife. We set off on a poor footing and I'd like to resolve our differences."

The other conversant entered his sightline: the gossip from the general store, Sally. She cast him a sour look. He supposed he'd broken her stride.

"My husband is away at the moment, miss, but I'll take your card," the pastor's wife said.

Leslie retrieved the envelope from his satchel. She was careful to pluck it from him without brushing fingers, as if avoiding contagion.

"Thanks again," he demurred with a honey-sweet smile.

Their combined attention weighed on him as he walked away, hoping the swinging skirt left an impression on the town chatterbox. None of the people in Spar Creek knew jack-shit about him before or after his arrival, and whatever they *did* believe about his mannishness or unsuitability could be countered with some effort. Disrupting their assumptions about him also provided a contrarian, catty pleasure. Any reaction was more useful than stonewalled silence.

The lengthy road back to the Hansall property carried him past the tobacco barns. The sounds of labor, thumps and calls and laughter, echoed from inside. He craned his neck and spied three familiar boys through the open doors, the blonds with the ginger, plus a smattering of men too old to have gone for the draft yet still spry enough for the barns. Worrisome though expected, he saw no Stevie. He knew close to nothing about the youth beyond poisonous rumors and his own projected sympathies, but there would be no forgetting what he'd witnessed. Maintaining a steady, patient presence around town would allow Stevie to seek him out if and when desired. Pursuing his official assignment gave him the cover to stay, and thereby a chance to offer his services.

On return, he discovered a notecard tucked beneath his cabin door that read: *Be my guest at supper tonight, you can stand in for Jackson. At the parsonage 7:30 pm. T Landsdale*

Though he left early Leslie was the last guest to arrive; Landsdale must've invited the other council members ahead of him. Missus Holladay, whose given name was apparently Ruth, gestured him into the parsonage without acknowledging either his previous visit or the missive he'd left for Holladay. A stilted chorus of greetings rose from the assembled councilmen and their wives, four men and three women arranged down the length of an oak dining table. Two seats had been left open, one to either side of Holladay. Leslie took the offered spot at the pastor's left. Ruth stood behind Holladay's chair and pressed his shoulder. The stakes felt higher and heavier than the surrounding mountains. Why were they allowing his presence at their table? What caused their change of heart, and what might it hide?

"Thank you for having me," Leslie said.

The man seated diagonally from him replied, "Of course. I was just reminding my fellows here how poor our hospitality has been considering you traveled all this way on our invitation."

Stillness enclosed the room, like a too-long held breath about to become a gasp. Leslie committed the man's face to memory: plainly freckled with a trim dark beard and green eyes. The woman at his side was equally average in her handsomeness.

"Brother Timothy reminded us of our Christian duty, and I admit we have been remiss," Holladay said. "Spar Creek did call for you, and so I've agreed to discuss whether your continued presence has any amenability with our beliefs."

*Continued presence* lay on the table between Leslie's folded hands and Holladay's splayed elbows, a coiled viper. No one else spoke. Leslie's thoughts flitted in search of a politic response—because he could not bear to be forced out now, without seeing properly to the Mattingly situation. While Holladay might intend to eject him, he wasn't the only person listening, and they'd given him a platform.

"The Frontier Nursing Service is itself a godly institution," he ventured. "Naturally, I would be quite surprised if we could find no grounds upon which we agree."

"That remains to be seen," Holladay said. Tipping his chin backward to his statuesque wife, he said, "Ruth, would you care to serve our guests?"

"Of course," she demurred.

Though smooth as butter, her poised speech struck Leslie as slippery too: something of the unreal in her performance as the ideal helpmeet. Her bearing as she disappeared into the kitchen, making no request for assistance, gave the impression of stiffness rather than strength. Perhaps he was projecting discomfort on a woman perfectly satisfied to be treated as a servant, but nonetheless, he disliked witnessing the exchange. The distaste he found when he met Ames Holladay's eyes matched and opposed his own.

"So you know," interjected Landsdale's wife with a conspiratorial lean, "I told these fellows it only made sense for you to wear trousers on the ride down from Hazard. Just look, you're in proper skirts tonight."

Leslie affected a laugh and shook his head once, as if embarrassed to discuss his dress habits. "Thank you, ma'am."

Ruth returned with serving dishes, laying the table with a pot roast and potatoes, stewed greens, biscuits, and creamed honey, delivered across a few trips. The Landsdale woman shot him an unexpected, encouraging smile beneath the preacher man's upturned nose; after a week of constant public rebuff and ostracization, the faintest sniff of approval hit him like cocaine. He needed allies, even the mildest sort.

"We shall say grace," Holladay intoned once his wife took her seat.

The elder gentleman seated next to Leslie grasped his clammy hand; Holladay took the other in a proprietary grip that made his skin crawl. Group prayers always made Leslie want to flee, but for the sake of passing amongst the godly, he shut his eyes and held on. His hands felt disconcertingly petite when engulfed by those of two adult men.

Holladay droned, "May the Lord bless this meal and guide us as we seek to understand his plan. I pray we join in fellowship as his light enters our hearts and staves off dark influences, as I beseech his Holy Spirit to come over the misguided children of Spar Creek. Please set them to rights once more with the gentleness of a father's hand. In Jesus's name, amen."

"Amen," Leslie echoed, though it stung his mouth like glass dust.

As they parted hands, Ruth gestured to the set table and said, "Please, help yourselves."

Platters circled, serving spoons clinking on dishware. Leslie claimed a reasonable portion of each offering, eyes on the women's plates to judge what he should take. Stress tied his stomach in knots, but the roast beef still made his mouth water. First bites were taken and savored with murmuring approvals before Holladay opened the floor to business, saying:

"Now, Miss Bruin. I understand from my wife that you called earlier to speak with me, but I'm sure we'd all like to hear: tell us what exactly your service intends for you to do here."

"The answer is twofold," he said, making earnest eye contact with each council member in turn. Had Ruth told her husband he'd overheard her gossiping, or no? Either way, he braced himself to deliver the FNS manual rhetoric—*eugenicist* rhetoric, if he was honest—that these people might be most receptive to. Battlefield nursing had been cruel to the soul but easy on the conscience; the Frontier Service was the opposite, sometimes. "Missus Breckenridge founded her philanthropic service to address mortality amongst mothers and babies in the counties. She believes the—the people of Appalachian stock have an intrinsic, godly understanding of the proper roles of husbands and wives, and sees it as necessary for our national health to encourage the . . . survival of those values through good breeding. Of course, the Kentucky boards task us with charity vaccinations, too. No one wants to see babies sick with typhoid, not when it's so easily prevented. For me, those vaccinations would be my first priority in Spar Creek."

The final point provoked a round of agreeable murmurs; even the two old men and their placid silent wives nodded. Leslie swallowed a surge of satisfaction.

Then Holladay said, "Charity inoculation is, perhaps, a good work. But on family matters I challenge you: How can a woman of your age, educated yet unmarried, possibly model the proper role for her sex? What could you offer a young wife that her mothers and grandmothers could not, beyond confusion?"

Riding the initial burst of acceptance, Leslie countered sharper than intended, "Well, sir, I offer my experience in field surgery. If the nearest doctor is two days' ride from the birthing bed, I bet that young wife would rather have a nurse than no one."

"No need to get feisty, Miss Bruin," Landsdale interjected. His chuckle was forced. Leslie buried the desire to fire back beneath a conciliatory smile. "We understand the dangers—we've lost babies here too. I suspect Brother Holladay is concerned with whether or not doctoring should come between a husband and wife, like prophylactics and such. We don't truck with all that."

"Then you'll be glad to know the nursing service doesn't offer anything of the sort," Leslie said.

Holladay cleared his throat and said, "I fear this discussion is becoming inappropriate for the ladies. Let us continue our meal in quieter reflection."

Leslie bowed his head, performing submission though the nape of his neck burned. Meat and potatoes quieted the table for several minutes. Ruth Holladay was a talented cook, regardless of the company she kept. The greens were rich with vinegar, peppers, and lard. Eventually, dribs and drabs of talk began to flow: a lost sow which the owner suspected had been stolen, a schoolyard tussle resulting in a broken nose, plans to extend the road and expand logging. The grey-haired gentleman to Leslie's left had a slurring baritone and inalterable convictions about lumber rights.

Council business was three-quarters holler gossip and one-quarter solutions. Leslie held his tongue, occupying the same speechless auxiliary position as the assorted wives. The only thing that kept him paying attention was knowing that at least one man at the table knew what violence had been done to Stevie Mattingly—but not a word had been spoken on the matter, neither concern for the offended party nor censure for the act itself. And so, he waited for an opportunity with all the patience he could muster. Finally, over slices of sugar pie leaking translucent across a blue plate, Holladay turned to him once more.

"I realize that as an outsider you do not, and could not, understand the magnitude of the forces at work here," he said in his preaching register.

Supper conversations stilled around them.

"What forces are those?" Leslie inquired.

"This town rests on an unholy land, Miss Bruin, and our people must constantly resist its darkness lest the town be lost. Our founders understood as much; to conquer and settle Spar Creek cost them dear. Have you not wondered why our hills are unmined and our woods left so wild?" Candlelight flickered severely across his face. "Satan's forces muster on our borders. Devils lie in wait to devour our weakest hearts. Not five years past, a woman burnt her house with husband and children barred inside. We are no city folk, sinning freely without fear of reprisal. Our feet rest on a knife's edge; I must be vigilant in guiding my flock from all forms of degeneracy."

"Amen," the oldest man said.

The remaining councilors echoed him, while Leslie reeled from his casual report of mass murder. Shaking off his recollection of eerie night whispers and the *presence* he'd sensed across the banks of the Spar, he said, "I don't disagree there is a strange air here, but what connection is there between medicine and these devils? Is doctoring itself not an exercise of god's dominion over nature?"

"It isn't the doctoring I object to, Miss Bruin, it's the impropriety of the person providing it," Holladay said.

His abrupt vehemence knocked Leslie back on his sit bones.

"Sir, what evidence of impro—" he began.

"We should debate the matter further amongst ourselves," interrupted Landsdale.

Leslie bit his flapping tongue.

"Aye, we surely will," grumbled the quiet man at the other end of the table.

"Council is thereby adjourned," Holladay unilaterally announced.

Leslie stuffed a bite of pie in his mouth before everyone else pushed their chairs back, rebuffed once again. Landsdale's wife rounded the table and tapped his elbow, murmuring, "Good effort, dear, but I suggest you see yourself home."

Ruth gathered the women to attend the dirty dishes; the men dispersed onto the porch. Leslie wiped greasy fingers on a napkin while Holladay loomed beside him. When he stood, the pastor laid his hand over the bony wing of Leslie's scapula. An old band of scar tissue itched at the contact, muted though it was. Sugar and buttermilk soured the spit he swallowed in anticipation of some petty, unwitnessed cruelty.

Except all Holladay said was "Be well," before guiding him out the door.

Landsdale and the older men on the porch had a cigarette and two pipes lit among them. Fat clouds of tobacco smoke wafted around their heads. Leslie inhaled, appreciative. Though he had every intention of heading on his way, the white-haired gentleman seated on the Holladays' rocker bench waved. Leslie paused at attention.

"I hear you served," the man said.

"Yes, sir," Leslie replied.

"Where and when?"

"I was stationed on the Marne," he said. "Near Reims, 'til the armistice."

Landsdale hissed with sympathetic understanding; sensing another possible opening, Leslie gestured to his jacket pocket.

"May I join you for a smoke?"

"Richard lost three sons in the trenches," the oldest fellow said, pointing to the other man. "But the nurses saved as many of our boys as they could. I say you earned that smoke."

Bloody memories spoke through Leslie as he said, "For our countrymen, we did what needed doing."

Richard offered him a match light and he puffed 'til his cig caught.

"Bless you," he said through his teeth.

Kitchen chatter floated on the breeze into their companionable quiet. Leslie caught one snatch of a phrase—*but what else did she expect to happen, sneaking around at night*—and damningly saw the men react: eyes sliding aside, legs jiggling, jaws rigid. Men for whom those words dredged an ugly truth forefront of mind; men who knew. Leslie sighed a milky lungful of smoke to the eaves, nerves at once afire.

"Do you need seeing home?" Landsdale asked.

Leslie looked across the moonlit yard, then back again. The bobbing circle of light rising through the porch lantern's bell turned the men to leering ghouls.

Through the lump in his throat, he managed, "No, I'll be all right."

# VI.

Leslie wrestled his fourth bucket from the well's pulley hook. The tub required a minimum of seven for an adult's bath. When he'd asked to borrow the bathing tub again the look Sarah had cast him seemed to say *Well aren't you spoiled, city girl.* In truth he needed a task for his idle hands. Once he'd scrubbed himself clean, he could also soap the dried sweat from his clothes. Hours of labor, settled. Through the process of hauling water, he listed missing comforts: flush toilets, warm showers, telephones, bookshops, working girls' clubs with bottled beer under the floorboards, a single solitary friend. Hansall hadn't returned from the mines, the council hadn't contacted him with their decision, and he felt distinctly as if he'd been placed under house arrest. The peculiar limbo had steadily intensified his nightmares. Lack of good rest left him grasping after shadows at the corners of his vision, and a strange gravity seemed to tug at him from the woods behind the cabin.

On the trail the night before, lantern held aloft and ears strained for the slightest sound, Leslie had admitted his position's precariousness. The state of play in Spar Creek had become clear: some people *knew,* but he couldn't be sure whom and to what extent, nor were those people seemingly aware of *his* encounter with Mattingly. The whole lot were inclined to prevent him from seeing what went on behind the town's godly facade. Their supposition of his ignorance lent him some room to maneuver, at least. Though he desired to march straight on over to the Mattingly household, the consequences of rash action wouldn't fall on his head alone. Hateful as he found the experience, he needed to be patient.

Hooves thudded on the packed dirt of the distant road, and then, Leslie realized with a jolt, the household lane. Chickens fluttered and squawked. Leslie refused to turn lest he seem too eager; he continued trudging along with the bucket in a farmer's carry, sloshing water across the toes of his boots.

"Hullo there," Jackson Hansall called cheerfully. "I have some mail for you, but I guess you've got your hands full!"

"Just a minute, yeah," Leslie grunted.

Hansall hitched the horse and trotted by him up the cabin stairs. He'd rolled his trousers to the knee. By the time Leslie hauled the bucket to the tub and dumped its contents, Jackson had dropped a package and two envelopes on his desk and begun examining his books. He tapped his fingers on the cover of Wilde's unexpurgated *De Profundis* and moved on. The uneasy thrill of passing such material under a devout man's nose wriggled—though *Orlando,* tucked beneath his pillow, was more titillating.

Hansall said, "By the by, I stopped over at Tim and Anne's, and he passed along a note about the meeting. Give it a read, tell me what you're thinking over supper?"

"I surely will," Leslie agreed.

Hansall parted ways with an understanding nod. Leslie listened as he swooped down on his kids for a tussle: squealing alongside the shouts of a father who only seemed to raise his voice for play. Nerves stopped him from opening the Landsdales' council letter; he needed to prepare himself first. Three buckets later, door barred and drape covering the open window, Leslie stripped nude. He combed fingers through the hair at his armpits and crotch, checking for ticks; with the mirror's assistance, he examined the scar-speckled expanse of his back, ass, and haunches. Sinking into cool water and scrubbing sweat-greased dirt from soles to crown fractionally settled his anxiety.

After dumping his clothes in for a soak, he snagged the letters from the desk to read by the window, appreciating fresh air on damp skin. The first missive had been forwarded from his boardinghouse, sent by a Tiffany Parsons from Oak Park to "dearest Les Bruin." The velvety-purple cursive read:

> *Addie told me last night that I hadn't been seeing your handsome mug around because you left town. And before I had the chance to say a proper hello, how dare you! So I thought I'd write a little and tell you I think you should have asked to buy me a drink. A photo is enclosed so you'll remember me fondly and maybe will call on me at home when you come back. I would surely enjoy the caliber of your company if our brokenhearted Lucy-girl is to be believed.*
>
> *Yours, Tiff*

The black-and-white wallet portrait stuffed in the envelope showed a cute, button-nosed woman with pale hair. Leslie made a reminder to thank Addie for passing along his address. Even if he never returned to the city or met sweet Miss Tiff, the flirtation smoothed his roughened edges like aloe on a sunburn. He doubted Lucy's heart was particularly sore, as she had given *him* the boot: his romantic performance was nothing to scoff at, she had assured, but his lack of spontaneity made her feel as though he were acting from a script. The critique still stung, in part because it wasn't unfair.

On the front, he'd been only eighteen; he had arrived without ever so much as kissing a girl. By the end of nineteen he was drinking through the shellshock in Paris while memorizing rules for proper inverts, to supplement and structure his innate erotic impulses: *Handsome, masculine things should practice finger dexterity. Don't let a pretty girl flip you, and never flirt with other daddies; they're your own kind.* How strange it had been, anticipating freedom inside his discovered identity and instead finding a new set of expectations. He struggled endlessly to keep a flame burning past the first few dates, tripped up by the discontinuities between the stories held close in his heart, his models for what an invert's life could or should be, and his inability to *fit* those expectations.

The second note was from the Landsdales, and read thusly:

> Thank you for attending the council dinner and for your careful explanations. After some debate our membership has reached an acceptable compromise: as nearly all of us would prefer to see the kids get their shots, the FNS through yourself may provide vaccinations within the nearest possible timeframe. The church and council are able to assist in getting folks organized however is fitting, but would prefer to see it completed within the following week, after which we'd request that your service here be finished. Could our plan for the vaccines be set to Friday, or Saturday? Furthermore, the pastor and us agree that Spar Creek needs no assistance as regards mothering and marital relations; while I understand that might be your core training, please endeavor to respect our wishes on the matter, or you'll be asked to leave sooner rather than later. Word does tend to get around these parts quick, be warned.

*The wife and I pray this compromise serves so as to not entirely waste your travel to our town. Be well,*

*Tim and Anne*

Leslie grinned flatly, neither pleased nor disappointed. While on the surface his work would be permitted to go no further than inoculations, what better chance could there be to reassess the townsfolks' measure and position himself accordingly? He had at the least bought seven more days in Spar Creek, seven more days for Mattingly to seek his assistance. He intended to milk the opportunity dry.

Lastly, there was the package littered with international freight stickers. An unfortunate thought occurred to him. He glanced at the locked door before slitting the tape. Just as he'd feared, ten petite rubber caps lay nestled in packing material with a receipt in French. The shipment of diaphragms he'd ordered to a fake name at the boardinghouse—but had not received in a timely manner, and so assumed confiscated by the postmaster—had, somehow and someway, been forwarded on to Hazard. With a cuss Leslie stuffed the contraband to the very bottom of his travel pack. If these were discovered, summary firing by the FNS would be the least of his worries. Perhaps another place might have been grateful for a stock of prophylactics, but as the Landsdales' letter emphasized, in Spar Creek those hidden helpers would get him run out of town—or worse. On further consideration he stuffed his pack beneath the bed. Out of sight, out of mind; seven days remaining to complete his mission.

Despite his best efforts, Leslie spied neither hide nor hair of Stevie Mattingly through the next five days. The boyish youth was absent from the church meeting house during Wednesday-evening sermon when, to a ripple of consternation, the councilmen announced their vaccination drive. He was nowhere to be seen while Leslie traversed the town pasting hand-lettered flyers at public gathering places: "Inoculations for All—Children and Adults—Whooping Cough and Typhoid and More—Schoolhouse Saturday All Day." He wasn't even in the tobacco fields with the men and boys, a detour Leslie made each afternoon. Neither had he overheard a single misplaced piece of chatter from the townsfolk, who had shifted overnight from ignoring his presence to being overly canny about it. He couldn't eavesdrop quite so easily, anymore, to gather what rumors might be passing from house to house in the evening social hours; he couldn't guess how much, or how little, knowledge of Mattingly's circumstances was circulating. What injuries, bodily and otherwise, might Mattingly have sustained—left five days to fester?

Preparations for the event had him both footsore and heartsore. Visiting each homestead involved endless walking. Though people might crack their doors for a reminder about inoculation day, their eyes remained coolly disapproving. The council's tepid, temporary backing wasn't sufficient to correct weeks of stoked hostility. Nonetheless he kept his fingers on the thready pulse of Spar Creek, alert and hoping for better fortune. His ever-present nerves barred him from easy sleep, however. Some nights he dragged the desk chair beside the door to sit awake, arms crossed and chin drooping to his chest, as the Spar carried on eerie conversations through the trees. Drifting thusly spared him from ugly dreams of dirt and blood and being held facedown against his will; he drifted instead through black, liquid warmth, as if the hills had swallowed him safe into their gullet.

Over Friday-morning coffee, Hansall said, "If you're feeling idle waiting for your big day, you could join us in the fields. The boys are down a set of hands and time's running short."

"Beg your pardon?" Leslie managed around a honey-soaked bite of biscuit.

"I heard Stevie's been unwell, maybe come down with something. Or, she had a bad row with her ma? With how tongues wag, you never know," he said—sunnily unbothered, as if he'd missed the memo that he shouldn't speak to Leslie about these matters.

Leslie caught the scent of opportunity. "Do you know if someone's gone around to check on them?"

"I suppose the pastor has," he replied.

Sarah hip-checked the kitchen door open, dish basin beneath her arm. Her eyes met Leslie's across the table, and while gathering the children's used plates she said, "It's not polite to mind other families' business."

Leslie supposed she, somehow, *knew*.

"Afraid it's in a nurse's nature to mind more than everyone else," he said.

Sarah nabbed his plate with the last bite of biscuit still on it. After she swept from the room, Hansall sighed and rolled his eyes. He seemed a good enough man, but the fact that he wasn't remotely concerned about his wife's displeasure with their guest was at once beneficial to Leslie and rather unflattering.

In a low voice, he asked, "Are the Mattinglys settled somewhere past Auntie Marge? I'm nearly finished dropping in on folks about the drive but haven't made it out there yet."

Hansall nodded. "The end of the road splits off toward them and the Pearsons."

"That's my day sorted, then," he said as if nothing unusual were afoot. "Give the tobacco my regards, and if you don't mind—"

"Pester the menfolk about tomorrow, yes, ma'am," Hansall finished.

Leslie saluted and stepped out onto the porch. The hound dog lifted his head, so he allowed the ol' boy to lick his fingers. Boots laced and calling cards at the ready, he mounted his borrowed horse to finally pay the absent Stevie his respects. He'd put the visit off long enough that, hopefully, it held no taint of the "interference" the council had forbidden. Traveling away from town during working hours meant Leslie was the only person in sight. On impulse he'd tucked the shard of fluorspar into his breast pocket, a ticket of safe passage over his heart. Passing the narrow path to the auntie's, he carried on to a pair of branching tracks as promised. The clearer one had a post painted with the name *Pearson,* while the other was unmarked, creeping with underbrush. Unsure what awaited him, Leslie hitched the horse to a tree. She lowered her nose to the ground in search of grass to crop. Leslie shook out one leg then the other to settle himself—flesh, spirit, and mind in agreement—before stomping down the path.

Even in daylight, a scummy film of shade lingered amongst the tangled saplings and brush. No blue glass hung from the branches overhead. Crows chastised him from the canopy as he broke the branches floating at eye level. Though the creek's babble was quieter on this side of the road, the pressure of the woods—its fetidness, the scuffling animals hidden from sight—outweighed even the intense aura encircling Marge's property. Trudging onward, Leslie tried to remind himself that the discomfort he felt was nothing more than electrical impulses in his brain, provoked by stress. The forthcoming conversation was bound to be unpleasant even without conjuring devils, and he'd be damned if he lent credence to a thing the preacher man said.

But he still couldn't help feeling observed.

He stumbled onto the Mattingly homestead without forewarning, a flat oval of cleared land holding a two-story square house with garden, outhouse, and pump well. Unlike the wilding path, the yard had been maintained. Chocolate-brown clapboards lent the house an imposing air. Without cats, dogs, or even a stray hare, the property seemed lifeless, but a twitching white curtain in the upper window proved it watchful. Army cap jammed into his armpit, Leslie climbed the porch stairs. He rapped his knuckles on the front door four times, then settled. However, while shifting weight from one heel to the other, a glint from the windowsill caught his eye.

Listening another moment but hearing neither footsteps nor voices, he sidled down to stand before the glass panes. On the other side, he saw an unoccupied kitchen—and along the length of the frame ran a neat row of nails sealing the window shut. Sawdust and paint flecks remained around the shiny iron heads. Gorge rising, Leslie strode toward the other end of the porch to check there as well, only to flinch harder than a spooked horse when the front door swung open.

"What is it?" an older woman asked, peering at him through a five-inch gap.

Leslie laid a palm over his thumping heart. He aimed for a winsome smile but fell short, stiff-cheeked. "Sorry, you gave me a scare. I thought no one was home."

Missus Mattingly said nothing, though when she shifted, the door rattled. The gap was held close by a chain strung at waist height. Around the woman's neck hung a woven twine cord that disappeared into her blouse. Her arms were sturdy from labor, her outfit plain and matronly, and she had pure hellfire in her face.

Unsteady, he asked, "Has the pastor come by to tell you about the vaccination drive, tomorrow, at the school? I heard your household has two members, you and an older child, and I'd be pleased to see you there. Or to deliver inoculations here, at your convenience."

"I've got no need of your services. Don't come back," she said—right before, as expected, slamming the door in his face.

Leslie sipped a breath through clenched teeth. The kitchen curtains swished closed, then footsteps crossed back past the door before Missus Mattingly yanked the other window covers as well. Already sure what he'd find, Leslie checked the second sill: another track of nails. Making a prison from a house meant blocking any possible escape routes. Missus Mattingly would surely claim safety reasons for women living alone on the edge of the woods, were she accused of mistreatment, but Leslie knew better. Turning his back on the house and leaving the property empty-handed struck him as an act of betrayal, even violence. The real and terrible question was, what on earth could he do? One last backward glance over his shoulder revealed a familiar, willowy frame silhouetted through the upstairs curtains, contemplating his retreat.

# VII.

Sleep had escaped to frolic with the night wildlife. Leslie sprawled over the desk chair, arms and legs splayed with the backrest dug between his vertebrae. The cabin ceiling fluttered with the furry bodies of moths. Fantasies straight from an issue of *Argosy* tripped over one another in his mind's eye: stealing a rifle and horse to enact a jailbreak, decrying the pastor and Missus Mattingly in the town square, using all the sneak-skills he'd learned at the front to find the culprit and rain justice down on his head. But practical considerations intruded on those heroic dreams. The vaccination drive had to come first.

Leslie collapsed forward to plant his elbows on the desk, dropping his skull onto the cradle of his fingertips. The muscles fanning from temples to jaw radiated tension. He massaged the ache down to his molars. He hadn't expected a holler post to be in any respect pleasurable. However, he had anticipated less animal *fear* than he'd already been feeling in Chicago, eyeing fascist flyers about Jewish influence and sexual degenerates while avoiding the cops who loitered around pansy clubs to check if people had worn the "correct" underpants. A rancid shift was blowing on the city wind, and Leslie recognized the scent; the stench wafting through Spar Creek differed in its specifics, but shared the same roots.

Despite the late hour he couldn't bring himself to strip down past trousers and undershirt, or to settle on the mattress. Neither could he focus on *Orlando*. The monotonous drone of battle readiness hummed at the join of his spine and skull. Vaccinations were arduous under ideal circumstances, and a restless night would do him no favors, but logic couldn't be reconciled with trained instinct. Pacing the length of the cabin—fourteen steps, turn, fourteen steps—was Leslie's only release.

In the middle of another endless circuit, the three-beat rap of knuckles on his windowpane flung him into a silent, cattish leap. It was past two o'clock in the morning. At another time and place, perhaps on watch for labor pangs, a knock near the witching hour would be normal. On the banks of the Spar it made his feet cramp. But duty called, and so he crept across the cabin and swiped the curtains back.

Stevie Mattingly stood on the other side of the glass. Ruddy-faced and wild-eyed, he glanced over his shoulder to the forest then made a sharp gesture at the window. Without hesitation Leslie pushed the swinging pane wide enough for Stevie to lift himself in. His boots scrabbled on the logs while all the muscles from his trapezius down to his wrists flexed. Leslie stepped aside, making room for the boy; his buttocks landed on the floorboards with an audible thud. Casting one searching glance along the tree line and seeing no further movement, Leslie shut both window and curtains. Stevie flattened his back against the cabin wall. His chest heaved.

They regarded each other warily. Sweat glued flecks of forest debris to his face and arms, his knees and trouser hems caked with mud. The brief downward bounce of Stevie's gaze made Leslie aware of his own thin undershirt, how the light clung to the bumps of his nipples and the furrow of his cleavage. Adrenaline fizzed, prompting a confused mixture of arousal and concern. *How did you get out?* he almost asked, but the possum-in-a-trap shine in Stevie's eyes stayed his questions.

Instead he pointed to the water pitcher. "Need a drink?"

"Yeah," Stevie croaked.

Leslie crossed the cabin, filled his glass, and brought it over. Stevie bolted the whole thing in four gulps. The distance between the Mattingly homestead and the Hansalls' by road was around three miles. Through the woods, whether on deer trails or fording wilderness, that trip would be quite the challenge—let alone in the depths of night. Stevie handed the glass back, Leslie refilled it, and the process repeated once more before Stevie crossed his arms over his bent knees. Though Leslie expected distress, he showed none—neither ducking his head nor wringing his hands. An impatient silence twisted the air.

"You're a nurse, and you know all the business of fucking," Stevie said.

Leslie slouched against the bedrail, agreeing: "I am, and I do."

Whatever question was due to come would be scouring in its delivery, he knew from experience. Stevie blew an aggrieved sigh between clenched teeth and pried himself upright on quivering legs. For the first time, Leslie spotted a bloodied scrape running the underside of his forearm to the elbow and a chafed set of bruise rings around his other wrist.

Without his needing to ask, Stevie said, "Used the bedsheets to climb out a window, but the knot slipped and I fell down the side of the damn house."

"Do you want a bandage?" Leslie asked.

He rotated the arm to glance at the depth of the wound. "Seems shallow, it'll be fine. But I'm—"

A convulsive swallow stopped him. Stevie dropped his arm limp at his side and glowered at the ceiling, like the moths were to blame. Leslie waited. The flush of exertion had left the boy's face and a sallow, white-lipped apprehension spread in its place. Another few calming breaths passed before he met Leslie's gaze again.

When he did speak, his voice was sure and steady: "It got me pregnant. I need that fixed, quick."

"Shit," Leslie said.

Stevie bared his teeth in a nasty smile. "I figured you'd get it. Late by the better part of a week. If I don't get it gone before someone notices, that's me wifed and done for."

*He's eighteen,* Leslie remembered with a cavernous panic. "I can't. I've got none of the tools with me, it wouldn't be safe, we'd need to go to the city—"

Stevie's incredulous laugh had a stabbing pointedness. One fist clenched while the other grasped for his belt buckle, as if he could wrench loose the violation planted beneath it. Rage poured from his posture, his grinding teeth and flexed jaw. His gaze darted around the cabin then landed with force on Leslie's stricken face.

"What good are you to me, then?" he bit out. "With what money and goddamn magic do I get to a city doctor, huh?"

"I could take you the day after tomorrow, I swear, if we just—"

He shook his head. "No, no. I should've known."

Stevie sidestepped his raised, imploring hands and made for the door, clearly less concerned with being witnessed now that his plan had failed. He knocked the bar aside and flung it open. Leslie followed on instinct, driven by the sympathetic horrors, but halted at the sight of Stevie's leap from porch down to yard. Chasing him would only be another act of disrespect.

"Wait, just wait a minute and talk to me. What're you planning to do?" he cried out.

Over a raised shoulder Stevie snarled, "Handle it myself."

Clouds passed across the moon overhead. Pitch night swallowed his rangy body without a trace. Leslie hissed, "Fuck."

Clusters of people milled around the schoolhouse yard and surrounding lane. The teacher's oak desk had been hauled onto the lawn, with two seats arranged beside it: one for the nurse, one for the patient. Sunlight slanted sideways over the hills and shredded mist rising from the trees. Coolness lingered in the bowl of the holler, but never for long. Within another hour or two the gathered folk would be fanning themselves and grumbling. Scattered throughout the loose crowd were familiar faces, including the Hansalls and council members plus their children and, presumably, grandchildren—with the notable exception of the pastor. A reasonable number of folks had arrived with kids in tow, more than Leslie had expected. Unsurprisingly, he caught sight of neither Mattingly.

On the heels of a sleepless night, the afternoon to come didn't bear thinking about. Exhaustion dragged down his eyelids, weighed on his fine motor control. He knew the numbness in his fingertips meant nerves were compressing under his swollen muscles. How was it that every single interaction with Stevie seemed to end with him standing slack-jawed in the boy's wake? Leslie felt worse than useless, and the council surely expected his departure within a handful of days once the vaccines were finished.

Over his shoulder the schoolmistress harped, "Aren't you ready yet?"

His tidy array of supplies—syringes, vaccine material, Band-Aids, alcohol swabs—was offset in professionalism by the fact of being outdoors on a desk. A parasol covered the workspace, keeping direct light off the case of vials. He had a job to do, and Spar Creek's children should not have to bear the costs of their parents' cruelty.

He said, "Ready as I'll ever be, ma'am."

She frowned. Her reaction to this use of her schoolhouse was downright combative. Leslie swallowed a sigh, then lifted his hands to his mouth.

"All right, who's first in line?" he shouted with as much enthusiasm as he could muster.

Owlish staring answered, from adults and children both. He gestured to the patient seat and smiled the best he could. Nudging from the council had perhaps brought people along, but it couldn't make them volunteer. The nearest family, with three children aged from baby to rangy teenager, shifted in place when Leslie glanced at them.

While he steeled himself to do a little friendly cajoling, the schoolmistress cut through with a saccharine edge, "You don't want to be inoculated, do you, children? It'll hurt."

"No," blurted a boy fretfully clutching his mother's sleeve.

Tongue flicking the word *shit* behind his teeth, Leslie glowered at the teacher, who smirked back. The energy of the crowd shifted as the youngsters became whiny, restive with the sense of having been trapped into something unwelcome. Swishing his skirts to the side and thumping with theatrical seriousness onto his chair, Leslie leaned an elbow on top of the desk.

"Miss Jones is a little scared, and that's okay, but surely one of you is brave enough? She could use some help, I think, from the bravest child in town."

A hush fell.

"I'll be second if somebody else will be first," called Hansall's oldest.

People glanced at one another to see who would jump for the chance. Sarah pinched her son on the ear, but softly, exasperated. Leslie wondered whether he had some quarrel with the teacher to prompt his streak of defiance.

"Can't let my boy show me up, huh?" said Jackson, tossing an arm over his son's shoulders. "I'll be your first jab, Nurse Bruin. Where do you want me?"

"Thank you kindly, and take a seat right there."

Once Leslie settled him in place, delivering his jabs in triplicate was the simplest task on earth. When his son's turn came, the boy bit his lip during the initial prick but steadied afterward.

When the last needle withdrew, he announced with puffed chest, "It didn't hurt at all, Miss Jones!"

"Why, thank you, Lucas," the schoolmistress said. Leslie narrowly avoided laughing at her frosty tone.

The townsfolk shuffled into a loose line, approaching the table in various states of apprehension and annoyance. Several babies cried and one toddler bit her mother, but otherwise the process went smoothly, if slow as chilled syrup. Disinfecting supplies, rotating which side he delivered injections from to avoid cramps, chatting down the more nervous patients: Leslie fell into a practiced rhythm, and for the first time since he left the Hazard train station, he felt something near relaxation. None of the slobbery, snot-nosed babes wrangled through the queue would cough themselves to death. That was worth his personal discomfort. Putting his hands to use once again reminded him of the reasons he'd joined the FNS, and the reasons he hadn't yet tendered his final notice.

People waiting their turn also seemed to forget, finally, that he might hear them murmuring amongst themselves. The bubbling of small-town secrets was just too pressurized for anyone to contain. While drawing up another dose, attention theoretically focused on the bored teenager waiting for her shot, he tuned his ears to the mutters amidst a gaggle of middle-aged parents.

"Did you hear? Delia Mattingly told the Holladays that Stephanie has gone and run off," said one gentleman.

"And the Marshall boy is still trying to court her," replied the woman at his side. She lifted a cupped palm as if to muffle her voice, and continued, "He's all in for that bearcat, who knows why."

"Expect a pinch in one, two, three," Leslie said.

"Ouch," the girl replied mildly as the needle sank through skin.

"Two more to go, and you're free," he said.

The man in the gossipy group shifted and the wind blew away his response; Leslie strained to hear, fumbling for the second vial. His patient swept her eyes over his face, back to Miss Jones presumably hovering in the wings, and then returned again. She leaned close to whisper: "—and *I* heard Stevie said she'd cut Floyd's prick off if he ever got near her again, after that first proposal."

Experience alone kept him from reacting bodily as the syringe plunger pulled clear, precious liquid into the chamber. He gave an acknowledging hum and pressed out the excess air before moving down her arm an inch. Two fingers resting on the crook of her elbow, he angled his chin down to hide his lips and replied, "That's a known fact, then?"

"Sure is, but he doesn't care," she said. Then she laughed and winced, performing nerves for the woman who must have at some point been her teacher through the second bite of the needle. "Oh, that one stings."

"Apologies, miss, but you're almost through," he responded, dull enough around the edges to sound tired but amiable. "Just one left."

"There's still quite a line waiting. Are you sure you can do them all today?" the schoolmistress groused.

"Yes, ma'am," he said, unhesitating.

No more conversation could be had, but he tucked that kernel of knowledge in among the rest. Whether swanning through city clubs or hidden away in quaint hollers, one thing stayed the same: girls kept tabs on which men were going to be trouble, and for whom. *Floyd Marshall.* After the third dose he passed the girl some Band-Aids, and she flitted away. The gossips had wrapped up their conversation by the time they arrived at his station. Inoculation continued as the sun passed overhead and the humidity rose to a sweltering pitch.

Several pitchers of water later, the line petered out. After the last patient came through, Leslie collapsed onto the seat and wiped his sweaty face clean with a rag. The muscles joining his forearms to his elbows had solidified into one big knot. However, on the horizon, he spotted a pair of folks trundling down the road: a man with a haul rope over his shoulders, attached to a cart seating one heavily pregnant woman. Her arms were crossed protectively around her belly, and her dangling feet nearly bumped the ground. As they approached Leslie stood. The woman was pale with exertion simply from sitting, and very young. Neither of the couple looked to be more than sixteen.

"How far along is she?" Leslie asked the boy.

"Eight and a half months, give or take." His jaw jutted out, but his expression was scared. "Aunt Jude said we didn't need your help or nothing, but she's in a bad way, and I figure it ain't wrong to ask."

"I can talk if you please, and my name is Beth," the girl snapped.

Leslie sketched a curtsy-bow. "Sorry, that was rude of me. How are you, Beth?"

"I'm carrying twins," she said without preamble. "And I can't hardly get out of bed. Mamaw is worried I might lose them or that they're too big for me."

Judging from the girl's size and carriage, Leslie was concerned the older woman spoke true. He said, "I can give you both your shots today, and I can make a house call to examine you where you're comfortable?"

"I doubt they'd let you inside," Beth replied.

Leslie glanced over at the grimacing Miss Jones. She tapped her wristwatch. The afternoon had wound down, and he suspected there would be no further takers. The echo of town chatter ricocheted between his ears, *Stevie ran off and no one knows where.* He'd intended to chase after Mattingly as soon as he finished inoculations, with the intent of getting him on the train to Louisville come hell or high water—given that his own excuse for remaining at Spar Creek had ended when he tendered the final jab—but he couldn't bear the guilt of turning away a pair of frightened, barely grown things who'd risked the council's censure to seek his help.

*One thing after the goddamned other.* Leslie strangled a cuss and said, "Can you make it down to the Hansalls' with that cart?"

# VIII.

Leslie arose from his nurse's cot aware that he was dreaming, remembering. The casualty clearing station stank of antiseptic and meat. The canvas walls held close their lantern's glow, safe as blackout curtains; by his bedside, on the ground, slept two younger nurses in a loose embrace. Slow-healing lacerations on his left thigh stung when he stepped over them. The tug of some invisible crook through his belly pulled him forward, past limply shivering boys—never men in the casualty tent, they were all boys praying to survive the night—who clutched one another's hands across the gaps between cots.

He'd left pieces of himself behind at those bedsides: with each futile dressing change over gas gangrene, each amputation, each dead teenager stretchered away, each farewell letter penned on behalf of the weeping ones who couldn't write, a chunk of his personhood had been excised. The numbness that remained made it easier for him to adapt, survive, endure; the situation in Spar Creek proved as much. The tent's flap toggle, when he reached it, was gore-sticky, slippery as a bullet lodged in someone's guts.

Outside he found himself stood in the middle of the Spar. The creek bed glittered under an orange harvest moon, stones blossoming from the earth like fairy circles. Trees rustled in chorus as if possessed by the desire to yank their roots free and go walking. The creek rippled against natural gravity, its current slopping and sloshing in whirlpools around his ankles. Jagged stones stung his foot-soles. Abruptly he understood himself to be nude, and his old war wounds began to ooze blood and lymph, feeding the muddy earth. Leslie knelt to press both hands against the stream bed. He buried his fingers within the gooey, sucking warmth beneath. His spine bowed, lowering his searching mouth to the Spar itself; when he plunged his tongue into richly salty water the pressure behind his eardrums popped.

Leslie woke panting and coated with sweat.

Booming thunder rattled the cabin. Rain roared across the roof in sheets. In the pitch darkness he felt certain that something immense, something hungry and terrible, had woken alongside him—dragged from his dream into reality. He fumbled to strike a match for the bedside lamp. Its faint glow encircled the bed, an island in the sea of night. Shadows lapped while he sat with quilt pooled around his waist and bare chest goose-fleshed.

The moment his heartbeat began to slow, a shriek ripped through the storm chatter. And then, it *continued.* Bleating screams jolted Leslie from his bed into his boots, but a gurgling silence fell as he lifted the bar from the door. He struggled to hear past the downpour and another artillery-tier thunderclap—but he knew, intimately, what death sounded like. He steeled himself. The last time he'd heard a noise outside, it was Stevie Mattingly coming to beg his help; the time before that, the same boy had staggered out of the woods grievously harmed. Leslie whispered a prayer: "Fucking shit, goddamn." He crept onto the porch and around the back of the cabin, lashed by rain and squinting through lamplight.

The doe's corpse waited near the trailhead. Guts strewn, hindquarters severed from torso, lower jaw missing. Leslie was backpedaling before the sight entirely registered with his conscious mind. Once barred inside the cabin, dripping puddles, he allowed the fear to pummel at his nerves. Whatever had done that damage, so quick and cruelly, couldn't be stopped by a mere curtained window.

Something had begun; something had changed. Static charge roiled through the holler, and though he couldn't guess its source, his bones felt its pressure. He waited for daybreak with knife in hand, remembering the unnamable things he had once thought he witnessed crawling between trenches. Alongside the gothic horror of nailed-shut windows and Spar Creek's taste for corrective violence, the nightmare and the mutilated deer unmoored him. He'd put a foot straight through the town's polished floorboards into festering muck. Sleepless and secret things hunkered down below, eager for an unwary stranger to fall through, but he'd never once abandoned a needful soldier, and the Mattingly boy would be no different.

Rapping on the door roused Leslie from a doze. The light through the curtains suggested he'd caught a few hours of rest after sunrise. Tossing his jacket over his undershirt, he padded across the cabin, expecting one of the Hansalls with breakfast or news. Instead, he swung the door open to find Ames Holladay on his porch. Leslie belatedly ran fingers through his tangled bedhead. Though he expected the pastor to shield his eyes from the intimate sight of his female body, Holladay stood straight with hands in his pockets. The height he had on Leslie felt more threatening than usual, an electric tension floating on the morning mist. The cold set of his face didn't help, either.

"May I examine your room?" he asked.

"Beg your pardon?" Leslie said.

"With your propensity for listening in on other people's conversations, I'm sure you're aware Stephanie Mattingly has run off from her mother's house. I'd like to confirm she isn't being harbored here," he said.

Leslie released an ugly snort, saying, "Have a look then, preacher."

He gestured into the one-room cabin: rumpled quilt and single desk, boots resting by the brass bedside. No space for a person to hide. Holladay nodded, accepting it as his due. Leslie badly wished to spit in his face. Insomniac nights whet his nastier edges, sanded down the numb facade to the readiness underneath. He'd spent long years practicing self-control for his own safety, strangling the urge to fight the kinds of men who claimed the blessing of *natural law.* Holladay was nothing if not that.

"Miss Bruin, as I understand it, you've completed your vaccination work," he said.

"With some measure of success, yes," Leslie agreed.

"Then shouldn't you be preparing your things to depart, as you've finished delivering inoculations?" The preacher didn't bother smiling. "Your willful meddling is neither needed nor welcomed—not with the Mattinglys, nor Beth Jacobs."

Cursory examination of the Jacobs girl had given Leslie real concern for her well-being. He'd spent the last light of evening setting up a supplies bag in case he was called on to assist her delivery, despite his pressing need to find Stevie. He bared his teeth in an expression far meaner than a grin. Holladay's regard stiffened with an aggression Leslie had to hope a preacher man wouldn't act on outright.

"With all due respect, sir," he replied, "you aren't my commanding officer, and you aren't the damned mayor. I have been exceedingly polite, and I have entertained your bullshit beyond my tolerance, but we have reached the end of that road. Get off my porch."

Holladay clapped a hard grip onto his shoulder, and Leslie bore it without flinching. "Please do reconsider. It'd be easier on all of us if you left before tonight, of your own free will," he said, mildly paternal. "Now if you'll excuse me, there is a sermon I must deliver on finding the courage to cast out wickedness—though I doubt I'll see you in the pews."

"You guess right," Leslie said.

Ames Holladay nodded once, clearly satisfied with his threat, and strode away through the mist. Leslie leaned against the doorframe. The flush of combat washed his nerves. If Stevie remained at large, he hadn't been imprisoned in the farmhouse again; however, Leslie had seen pure desperation lead to self-injury and abortifacient overdoses often enough to be worried about the boy "taking care of it himself." There was also the unfortunate doe, savaged to pieces on his doorstep. Leslie shuddered. Since Stevie had been so resistant to heading for Louisville, and since he'd heard of no horses gone missing, Leslie had to assume he remained around the Spar *somewhere.*

For the time being, he penned a few short letters: one to his FNS bosses, one to Addie, and one to Lucy, his last lover—whom he hoped, despite their separation, would give a damn if he died. Within each missive he named Ames Holladay, explaining that he'd been threatened, ordered to leave town, but intended to stay and see to the Jacobs girl as she neared the end of a risky pregnancy. He wasn't lying, but neither was he giving the entire truth. Then, he entered the Hansalls' house and pulled Jackson away from church preparation to inform him of the deer carcass: how close its death had been to the cabin, how gruesome.

"Shit, might be a panther," he murmured, casting a look at his rowdy kids. "I'll tell Sarah and the young'uns to keep out of the woods. You've shot before, right?"

Leslie rolled his eyes, affecting normalcy.

Hansall grinned in response, as anticipated. "Of course, veteran. I'll loan you a rifle for nighttime then. How much longer are you hanging around?"

"Much obliged, and I suspect a couple days more, just to catch any stragglers," he equivocated. "Say, are you heading to town again soon?"

"This afternoon after service, yes'm," he said.

Leslie passed over his three letters. "Would you mind? Business correspondences, reporting back on the vaccine drive and when to expect my departure, supposing I'll go on once you get back."

"Sounds sensible," he agreed without an ounce of suspicion. "Are you joining us for the sermon?"

Sarah glowered watchfully from the other side of the house, fists clenched in the rag she scrubbed the tabletop with. Aware of her ears and eyes, Leslie replied, "The last couple nights I haven't slept a wink, so I'm going to be a bad Christian and catch some rest."

Hansall chuckled, understanding. "Sneak some bacon first, before it's gone."

---

The trail crossed the burbling width of the Spar and continued on into wilderness. With the majority of the population at Sunday sermon, Leslie could finally explore the backways unobserved. Given the time crunch, he regretted his prior squeamishness around the deeper woods. Lord knew Stevie had emerged from behind his cabin often enough to assume the paths led *somewhere*. The strange dream from the night before lingered, recalled by the shimmering scattered mineral shards: how the musky, salt-lick creek water had dampened his mouth and chin, the eruption of psychic force that startled him awake. Try though he might to pretend otherwise, Leslie was a superstitious person, someone who'd seen and survived more than he should've. The woods, to his tender nerves, felt altered: hungrier, as if the branches reached for his face and the earth rose to meet his boots. The thrumming vitality was neither welcoming nor threatening—it simply *was*. Organic pressure kneaded at Spar Creek's borders, wriggled against its homestead fences.

Leslie flexed his fists and waded into the creek. His boots stirred silt and displaced minnows; a bee bumped against his cheek, bumbled nosily over the white cotton of his short-sleeved blouse. His wary eyes and ears made nature's calm seem almost artificial. As he set out along the second half of the trail, a white-tailed deer flitted through the foliage in the distance, but he saw no sign of other humans. After a half hour's hike the path split: one leg led farther into the wilderness while the other—broader, more traveled—curved back toward town. Fleetingly, he thought of Frost, and it brought a smile across his face. He'd follow that road not taken on the trip back.

Within another quarter of an hour, the rush of water grew louder. Between the twisting of the trail and the turning of the creek, he was once again on the opposite bank of the Spar—and across the stream, blue glass hung from the trees. Bottles dangled from twine loops; discs and shards littered the ground amidst the stones. A hunch he'd been carrying in the back of his head leapt to the forefront. He sped his pace.

The path spat him out on the edge of Auntie Marge's garden, where the woman stood gathering vegetables with a basket on her hip. Her gaze flicked across Leslie as if he were a regular visitor.

"You haven't left town, then?" she asked.

"No, ma'am," he said.

She sucked her teeth and popped an okra pod loose with a practiced twist. Leslie stuffed his hands in his pockets. She'd surely acknowledge or dismiss him as she saw fit, so he stood patient on the property line while she plucked the prickly bushes clean. Morning sun glared straight into his squinting eyes, until Marge loosely gestured *c'mere.*

"Carry this basket up to the house for me," she said.

The auntie passed her bushel of tomatoes, okra, and zucchini into his outstretched arms—heavier than expected given she'd been bracing the weight single-armed. The back door stood wide, allowing airflow through a screen. He passed beneath the lucky belly of the horseshoe nailed to the lintel. Bundles of drying herbs and flowers, some he recognized and some he didn't, decorated the rafters. Marge's poise eased his worries a fraction as she crossed through her kitchen.

"Put those on the sideboard and sit your butt at the table," Marge said.

Leslie did as he was told while she hustled a jar down from the cupboard and poured a draft from the gold-brown pitcher of sun tea steeping in the window. The table was sturdy under his elbows, hewn from its parent tree with the divots intact but sanded and polished to a sheen.

"I came to ask about Stevie," he said.

"I assumed as much," she replied, "though like I said before, I'd prefer to be left out of it."

Leslie took one sip: bracingly sugared. Marge folded her arms on the tabletop, a palm on each strong biceps. With her set square jaw and braided grey hair, she could've passed for a commanding officer in the nursing corps or a boss behind the bar at a girls' club. Though loneliness often made him seek kinship where none was to be had, the fact that Marge was at home doing chores instead of going down to church gave him a good feeling.

"I understand, but times are desperate," he said. "Do you know where I could find her, now?"

"Don't go asking how I know, but I gather you couldn't provide the needed service on short notice," she said.

"I didn't say no, but . . ." Leslie began.

"Listen. This trouble has been a long time coming," Marge said. "Twenty years ago Spar Creek was as decent a place as any for a child to be strange, but things change. Preachers preach and people get to whispering. Now it's coming to a head, and I don't know that Mister Holladay is prepared for what he has helped to unleash by pushing that girl over the edge."

"What do you mean?" he asked.

An orange cat leapt onto the table, meowing. Marge stroked from its nape to the flicking tip of its tail. She said, "If I told you a reckoning is coming, would you keep out of its way?"

"I'd rather help," he said.

The faintest smile turned her lips.

"Be patient, then, and ready to be swift," she said.

A booming knock on the front door echoed through the house. Leslie jumped, but the auntie did not, and neither did her feline companion. From the porch someone called, "Hullo there, Miss Marge!"

"That'll be the church posse again, searching for our wayward child," she muttered. "Stay quiet, and leave from the same door you entered through."

*Church posse,* Leslie mouthed.

Marge rose from her chair and flicked her fingers goodbye. He abandoned the glass of tea three-quarters full, slipping from the house and scuttling through the gardens. Credit to the horseshoe magic, none of the searching men came 'round the house before he escaped into the woods, but their rousing conversation echoed on his heels far closer than was comfortable.

The auntie had assisted Mattingly with something, perhaps several things, against self-interest. Remaining in Spar Creek, at clear risk to himself, was Leslie's own version of Marge's intervention. After years of foreign war, followed by police raids and bailing girlfriends out of jail, what remained of his moral center was dedicated to those of his own kind. The queerly willful creatures of the world had only one another to rely on. Whatever else young Mattingly could become, were he granted a future, he was surely willful; he'd rescued himself once already. But Leslie still needed to *find* him before the townsfolk worked up their courage to run off their undesirable nurse. Being caught alone in the woods would be a poor showing, though, as he'd just lied to the Hansalls about resting in their cabin.

Leslie detoured through the underbrush, creeper vines tangling his ankles. Somewhere behind, the posse hollered Stevie's name. Had the pastor told them Mattingly was lost in the woods, in a strop with his mother? Maybe a few knew the truth—maybe all of them did. While fording the Spar again, this time off the beaten path, he noticed an obscured branching track on his left. Glancing over his shoulder to be sure he was alone, he rustled the brush he'd disturbed into a more naturalistic arrangement and took the secret trail. The underbrush showed few signs of incursion: an errant footstep punched through a fallen branch, a rock rolled aside to reveal fresh black dirt beneath, a chalk hatching marked at the base of a tree trunk. As he carried on, an entrancing gravity began to tug behind his stomach; he couldn't determine if it was simple curiosity, or something heavier—something external, drawing him along.

The forest whispered around him with a thousand holy mouths. As Woolf had written, *Everything, in fact, was some-*

*thing else.* While he was distracted by the breadth and height of a stunning old oak that rose from the earth dead center ahead, its roots dotted with chunks of fluorspar, Leslie's right boot heel slipped into open air. He crashed, flailing, to his knees as the spell drawing his steps forward shattered.

"Fuck!" he blurted loud enough to flush a hare from the bushes.

Under his dangling foot yawned the mouth of a sinkhole, obscured by flowering honeysuckle. Though its grade wasn't steep, the cavern pulled like the void, the same as a cliff's edge. Leslie choked down his gorge and, ass firmly planted on the ground, eased past the blanketing vines into its maw. Before the darkness swallowed him, he struck one of the stove matches from his pocket.

Surprisingly, the alcove was no larger than a bedroom. The earth under his scooting elbows was rich and loamy; roots curled across the low ceiling. On the far side of the den hollow was an outcropping of limestone forming a natural shelf. Painted ideograms decorated its length, unreadable for the most part—aside from dozens upon dozens of hastily scrawled, consuming black eyes. A cold grip torqued his belly. The bloodthirsty chunk of spar in his breast pocket throbbed like a second heart, warm as life. Leslie waved the match flame nearer the altar, chasing back the darkness. Nestled on a gore-soaked bed of wishbone flowers, ringed with coal and snakeskin, lay a pale pinkie and ring finger severed at the middle knuckle.

The match sputtered out.

# IX.

Leslie staggered, pale and wheezing, from the forest—and almost ran straight into Sarah Hansall. She stood stone-faced with a rifle in her hands behind the cabin, gaze trained on the path. Though the barrel was pointed toward the sky the sight of the weapon nearly burst his jackrabbiting heart. He barely recalled his flight back, possessed by terror and near-religious awe, creeper roots snagging around his ankles. The echoing shouts of the posse had sped him on faster than the fresh-snipped fingers.

Sarah allowed the awkwardness to drag on before she asked, "Where'd you sneak off to, then, instead of attending sermon?"

"Couldn't sleep, thought I'd go for a morning constitutional," he managed. Sarah raised her brows in disbelief. "I heard . . . something, tracking me through the underbrush."

"Being a little too brave, aren't you," she said.

"You just saw me running, ma'am, so I don't know how brave I was," Leslie replied.

"That isn't what I was referring to," Sarah said.

She stroked a strong hand across the stock. Cheery birdsong merged with distant shouts, carried on the rustling murmur of the Spar. Leslie watched her finger slip through the narrow iron ring of the trigger guard. Neither her children nor her husband were here to bear witness; she had confronted Leslie alone.

"Jackson already left for town," she said quietly. "Since he wasn't sure how long you'd be rambling, he said to tell you the gun was yours until he gets back."

She circled and rubbed the trigger. Leslie couldn't tear his gaze away; hair rose from his neck on downward, and he said through a dry mouth, "Thank you kindly."

"The other message I aim to pass on is from the Jacobses, whose missus entered a prayer request at sermon today, and that is: How *dare* you let that idiot boy drag Beth across town and get her agitated?" The bile in her voice yanked his attention from her hands to her fury-pinched expression. "If she loses those babies, it'll be because you disrespected the one rule your trifling self swore to follow."

Leslie frowned. He said, "All due respect, ma'am, we're both after a healthy and safe delivery for Beth. The exam had me worried about her prospects, and with twins—"

"Just get the *hell* into that cabin, Miss Bruin," Sarah said.

"Come on now," he began, shifting on his feet.

"Hush your mouth," she said. "You've caused enough trouble, the pastor and all of us agree. You're to stay on this property and keep from bothering anyone else until either Jackson comes back to escort you, or someone finds Miss Stephanie and brings her home."

Sunlight glinted off the barrel resting across Sarah's shoulder. He scrounged up the pride to meet her eyes, nod his head in acknowledgment, and walk right past her onto the cabin porch without another word.

Behind him, she said, "My work will keep me around the yard this afternoon, but come sunset, I'll leave this rifle on the porch. Should keep you safe, supposing there is a real panther after all." A pause. "I've got another for myself in the house, of course, should it become . . . necessary."

Only after he'd barred the door against her did the shakes wrack him. He'd gotten too cocksure after sending those letters and, theoretically, buying himself a few more days in town. He experienced a guilty moment of frustration that the Jacobs girl had come to him, though she must've known the trouble he'd get in—followed by a wash of anger that she'd fallen pregnant so young at all, and that his assistance had been barred. Some letters dropped in the mail wouldn't prevent a bullet to the head, even if they led to justice for his corpse.

How on earth he intended to locate Mattingly now, let alone spirit him off to safety, he hadn't the foggiest. Perhaps the auntie would pass along a message, but otherwise he was over a barrel. For an hour or so, he listened to the metronome swing and thud of logs being split outside his cabin-slash-jail. Picturing an axe blade streaking through the air made his bladder weak. He hadn't given enough credit to the threat presented by Sarah Hansall, and that was simple mannish idiocy.

He tried to distract himself with the Woolf novel, but his mind continued to wander. Eventually, dusk drifted down the hillside beyond the window he'd left propped. He braced his elbows on the desk, pressed thumbs on either side of his jaw. Minutes later a rapping drew his attention to the door; he opened it to discover the back of the boy child retreating across the yard, a plate of braised venison in gravy with potatoes and carrots abandoned on the stoop alongside the promised rifle and partly empty box of ammunition.

The back door of the house hung open, Sarah standing backlit in its mouth. She ushered the child beneath her arm and shut them inside again. Leslie bent over for the plate, stomach rumbling after an entire day nibbling trail crackers from his otherwise barren supplies bag, though the meat smelled gamey. Darkness hadn't laid over the holler quite yet, but once it did . . .

he considered the rifle, his lantern low on oil, and the biding woods. For the moment, though, he sat cross-legged on the mattress with supper at his side and the final chapter of *Orlando* open on his knee. Relentless tolling clocks and baths of phosphorescence had begun to subsume the hero, or heroine, or hero; he read by the disappearing sun, nibbling through his vegetables. The phrase "at the back of her brain (which is the part furthest from sight), into a pool where things dwell in darkness so deep that what they are we scarcely know" rocked Leslie stem to stern. The strange cavern, and the ancient oak astride it, crossed his mind's eye.

The faint thud on the window almost failed to register—then all at once, his brain interpreted the signal from his ears correctly. He leapt from bed, tripped over the quilt, and flung aside the curtains. Stevie Mattingly, hair in a ratty knotted braid and dirt on his face, crossed his arms over the sill. One hand hid beneath the opposite elbow. He sported an arrogant and awfully handsome grin. He hadn't needed to be *found* after all—he'd been racing along on his own ventures while Leslie sputtered in first gear. Leslie stood gape-mouthed for a long second before dragging the pane aside and hissing, "Christ, get in here before someone sees."

"Don't worry yourself about that, or the *other* thing from before." Winsome, he ducked his head and smiled again. "Aunt Marge said you came by all worried for me, plus that you got in hot water when you told the preacher to go fuck himself, so . . . I suppose you're owed an apology. For me acting like a right little bastard, and getting you caught up here."

The stitch of worry cramping his abdomen popped loose. The pair regarded each other, a sweeter tension on the air. Something had changed.

"Where were you—" he started, at the same time Stevie asked, "So, what's that book?"

*Orlando* was still clutched in Leslie's fist. He held it aloft as if he'd never seen it before. Stevie tapped his fingers on the wooden sill, patternless noise, and cocked his head. A certain daring flowered in the space vacated by his earlier defeat. Leslie rushed to explain, "Well, it's a novel about . . . an immortal person who begins as a man, and then becomes a woman, and romances other men and women. The writer dedicated it to her lover, Miss Vita Sackville-West."

"Huh. Who'd have thought, being a man and a woman at the same time?" Stevie replied, husky.

"Me, for one," Leslie said. Stevie flashed him a crooked grin, which encouraged him to continue, "And I must assume you, too?"

"A bold question." His gaze swept Leslie from bobbing throat down to crotch, framed by the windowsill at the height of his hands. But then he said, "I did tell you to leave town before, but it bears repeating. What's coming next isn't your fault or your business, and you've caught enough trouble from these fuckers, yeah? Seen ol' Missus Hansall threaten you good, earlier."

Rough sentiment, delivered in a nigh-on friendly tone. Conspiratorial, even.

"And what *is* coming next?" he couldn't help asking.

Lantern light flared in the depths of Stevie's eyes when he blinked: the illusion of tapetum lucidum. Leslie swallowed reflexively.

"Come around town square tomorrow at high noon, if you really want to see," he said.

Commotion arose from the main house, children laughing their way to the outhouse before bed, and without another word Mattingly slipped away. The woods swallowed him whole in an instant.

Consciousness hit Leslie with blunt force. The lantern had gone out, and the darkness held a slithering heaviness. *Something* had rung his sleeping brain to alert. He lay silent as a corpse, blood thudding in his eardrums and throat. The rushing creek and croaking toads carried on innocently. No footsteps creaked the floor; no breath stirred the air. Through a squint he saw only blackness, except for the box of translucent curtain over the window, emitting the faintest moonlit glow.

A shadow passed across it.

Leslie swallowed his yelp. The fear bubbling inside him was at once a child's fear, monsters under the bed waiting for unsuspecting toes to dangle, and an adult's fear: townsfolk riled by a nasty sermon, or a man with bad intentions. An airy thump landed on the porch; weight groaned across the boards. Something pawed, scratching, at the wooden door. He remembered the dead doe with her absent jaw and spilled entrails. Logic told him the creature must be on the prowl, drawn by his scent and warmth inside the cabin. Surely no more than a panther, as Hansall had suggested. The shake of Leslie's fingers as he struck a match for the bedside lamp suggested otherwise. Survival instinct yowled from his guts loud as an air-raid siren.

The rekindled lantern revealed nothing on *his* side of the barred door. Another electrifying scrape dragged across logs on the backside of the cabin, as if the thing were marking territory. Leslie thought of the Hansall children asleep in their beds across the yard and the possibility that Sarah might've left windows cracked.

"Fuck," he subvocalized.

Before the front, he hadn't been a hunter; after, he attempted to forget the kinds of quarry he'd once bagged. He eased off the brass frame by increments to prevent it from squealing. Crouched in the shadows, he laced his boots and stuffed his ears with two bulbs of wax. Bodies remembered their routines: rifle strap over the shoulder, its bolt thrown ready, and three additional bullets tucked from the box into his pocket. If he needed a fourth reload, he had bigger problems. He stood beside the door and waited for it to pass by again.

When it did, whatever cast the odd silhouette—liquid and elongated—was far too tall to be a panther.

Leslie flung the door wide and shouldered the rifle with one breath. He flowed down the steps on muscle memory, searching for motion through the sights. A darkly iridescent, bulky shape separated from the side of the cabin. With no hesitation Leslie fired at its center mass. The rifle report shattered the night silence, hardly muffled by his earplugs; his skull rang, hands already reloading while the humanoid mass surged toward the trees. By the time he raised the barrel again, a second or two later, the thing was gone—melted back into the safe cover of the forest, a shadow made flesh that had dissolved once more. Leslie dropped the stock from his sore shoulder and stared into the woods, his pulse careening. Scoff though he might at the preacher man's demons, he'd seen—or, *imagined* seeing—things other than men rising from the muck on the front lines. Spill enough blood on it, and the earth was bound to go strange. As if he hadn't enough to deal with in this godforsaken town.

*Town square at high noon,* Mattingly had said.

Jackson Hansall wasn't back from town. His wife sat on the front porch, watchful, and her spine straightened when Leslie rounded the corner of the house.

"Easy, ma'am," he said before she could get fired up again. "Only going to the general store to lay in provisions for the trip back home. If you're so worried you could come on with me, I suppose."

"No," she said slowly. "That's all right."

Her face telegraphed suspicion. Leslie stood with hands in his skirt pockets, head cocked, projecting *don't want no more trouble* with every ounce of his being. Had she heard the rifle fire, the night before, and figured he'd been scared by some animal in the dark?

"Come straight back here," she said.

"Of course," he agreed.

Once his boot heels met the road, though, a mixture of anxiety and relief wracked him. His strategies for passing seemed near useless against Spar Creek's willful immiseration. Strangers on the road radiated open hostility. On his arrival at the town center, minutes before noon, the folks meandering through their errands gave him a wide berth. As expected, the Sunday sermon had evaporated what measure of goodwill he'd earned through inoculations. Mattingly hadn't arrived on the scene, and so Leslie escaped the street through the general store's creaking screen.

Judy Ellis peered at him over the top of her ledger. She said, "Brother Holladay told us you'd be heading out of town forthwith. Do you need some travel supplies?"

The premonition of a row charged the air.

"Well, my intention is to go once Mister Hansall returns, ma'am," he said, roundabout. "Came for some provisions in the meantime, seeing as he hasn't yet."

She closed the ledger. Her thin mouth smiled. "Unless you're readying your horse, today, I don't have stock to sell you."

"Come now," Leslie sighed.

"Go on, then." She flicked her fingers toward the door. "May the Lord Jesus bless you."

He spun on his heel, and a commotion kicked off suddenly outside: shouts and slammed doors, dogs yodeling. Leslie hurried onto the porch with the shop mistress close behind. Ames Holladay stood dead center in the road, maroon about the face and jabbing a finger at Stevie Mattingly, who'd planted himself shoot-out opposite. It seemed like half the town gathered 'round to watch the confrontation.

"Give the name of anyone else would go so far to spite me," the preacher spat.

Stevie had knotted the dark fall of his hair at the base of his skull. Dressed in shirt and trousers, hands in his pockets and work boots polished to a shine, he made a respectable young tough. The wildling woodsman was nowhere to be seen. Spar Creek held its breath as he tipped his chin backward in a performance of consideration—before forcing a brittle, braying laugh.

"You're always blaming me for something or other, so what should I care." He paused for effect. "Though, pastor, it makes me wonder: What could you have *possibly* done to someone that would make them wanna dump a carcass down your well, huh?"

Holladay had gone flush with anger. "Be still your tongue, slattern."

The calm facade sloughed from the plane of Stevie's raising shoulders. Leslie gripped the porch rail, suspended on his toes, ready to leap if a brawl were to break loose.

"Ames Holladay, I was born here in Spar Creek, and you sure as shit were not." Tension wrenched Stevie's measured tone down to a growl. Judy gasped under her breath at the profanity. "You didn't find me in the forest because I didn't *let* you. The dirt knows me, the trees know me, the creek knows me. These people have known me since I was born, and you—"

"None of that will stop you from bringing down damnation on their heads, with your sin, and iniquity, and witchcraft!" the preacher man interrupted with his church bellow. "Your own supposed neighbors, their cattle slaughtered and their wells poisoned, the streams running backward!"

"*Fuck you*," Stevie yelled right over top.

Holladay's momentum crashed to a shocked halt. Stevie whirled around to face the crowd, arms spread in supplication, wearing his field gloves despite the temperature.

"I came here to demand justice." One hard tremble shook his words. "I've been trespassed on, and that man there didn't give a damn after he was told. So grant me a measure of that righteous, godly justice y'all are so big on these days."

"Loose women cannot be trespassed on, especially not when they place themselves directly in the hands of men," Holladay intoned toward Stevie's back. He did not see Stevie's expression as the sentence struck, but Leslie surely did. Whispers poured from person to person but no one lifted their voice in his defense. Leslie bore the cool, steady weight of Stevie's gaze while his public appeal foundered, and so he caught the tiny flash of teeth before the boy faced Holladay again: like this was his plan all along.

Stevie said, "Well, if that's how you're going to be, then you've earned what you get."

"You do not know what monstrousness waits to piggyback your weak spirit," Holladay countered. "But you can still be forgiven. Rejoin the path of the holy before you damn us further."

"You damn yourself, preacher," Stevie said—then turned his back and walked away.

The crowd split to allow him passage between the buildings, toward the distant forest, silently flinching from either his bared teeth or their own guilt. Leslie found himself staring straight into Holladay's thunderously hateful eyes.

"And you," he shouted over the crowd. "What part of this rebellion and devilry is your doing?"

What felt to be one hundred eyes locked onto Leslie. Fear-parched from lips to stomach, he croaked, "None that I know."

Holladay scoffed. The townsfolk rustled, one organism.

"Spar Creek does not desire your presence, Miss Bruin. Pack your things and leave."

An ugly silence carried, hung fire. Leslie waited, taut as a wound spring, until the preacher shrugged his shoulders like settling a coat. By his side, Judy Ellis blew a quick breath. Without another remark Holladay also turned his back to them before striding away—a dismissal. Leslie scanned the crowd for a friendly face and spied none.

Satchel clutched at his side, he beat a retreat on Mattingly's heels. It no longer seemed to matter much whether the neighbors perceived some improper connection between them; the battle lines had been drawn, and he'd chosen the natural side. Leslie couldn't be bothered to find a trailhead as he suspected the boy hadn't either. Instead he forged through unkempt brush straight from the main road, eager to escape the public square. After some long minutes following a faint trail of busted branches and scuffed dirt, he saw a flash of color through the trees ahead. The creek beckoned with its constant murmur, and so he had to be approaching the familiar areas behind the Hansall homestead, though from another angle. Leslie crept close enough to discern, through the leaves, the contours of freckled shoulders and glossy dark hair bent over the water.

Before he spoke, the person said, "Ain't it rude to peep?"

"Stevie," he sighed, pushing through brush.

On the banks of the Spar, the boy squatted, his feet and chest bare. A small pile of mineral fragments rested nearby in the loop of a ground-burst root, space cleared to bathe. Stevie stood and stretched, lifting damp hands overhead. Water rolled from forearms, to biceps, to armpits, and finally onto small breasts tipped with coral-brown nipples. Freckles scattered every inch of his torso, ranging in color from pale tan to rich earth. Leslie foundered at the sight of him nude to his trousers and bothered not a whit by the commotion he'd left behind.

"How come you followed me?" Stevie asked.

"What else was I going to do?" he replied, exasperated. "Hard to say which of us those folks are madder at."

"We barely know each other."

"If that won't stop them, I don't see where it should stop me either," Leslie said, hovering as the boy stepped from the creek onto the muddy bank.

Dirt squelched between his bony toes. Scrapes ran across both elbows and the left side of his rib cage, but the minor wounds lent him a sense of careless confidence. More notably, the last two fingers on his right hand were absent below the knuckle.

"Quite the naturalist, aren't you," Leslie said.

"Honest to god, if they'd leave me alone, I'd make a house out here. I do fine without those people, but don't seem they do fine without keeping an eye on me. Fuck 'em." He hocked and spat. "What keeps you chasing after me, though?"

"Why not get away from here," he blurted. "Come with me, when I leave."

Stevie settled his butt on the big root, humming. He patted the spot beside him until Leslie sat, close enough to feel his warmth. The humid intimacy reminded him of bathing with the other nurses over a basin outside their tents—except he was overdressed.

"Why should I leave all this glory?" he said with a gesture to the woods. "I'm not letting a couple idiot men run me off, not when I could get rid of them instead."

Leslie stretched his legs until his boots touched the Spar. Stevie acted as if it weren't the whole town at issue, but he figured otherwise, though he couldn't find the words to say it. Instead, he said, "For one thing, because it's . . . a lot easier, safer, to be things like us in the city. There are other fellows to watch your back, and plenty of girls to run around with, if you want."

"What does that mean, anyway? *Things like us,*" he parroted.

Leslie gnawed the edges of his tongue. He'd done this chat before, several times, but it never got easier. There was a fine line between presuming too much and assuming too little, between what you guessed a person knew, or felt, or thought—and what they really *were* inside. Or, what they could be, given the language and opportunity. City-born, he'd always had access to books and strangers whose appearances caught his errant imagination on the street; he assumed Stevie, inventing himself from scratch in the holler, had not.

"Some people use the term invert," he explained. "A sort of

mirror-sex: the soul of a man in the body of a woman. Or *friend of Sappho,* that's girls who go for girls; sometimes around the bars, they'll say lesbian—"

"Lot of fancy words, that is," Stevie said. His fingers worked a piece of lavender spar between them, flashing sunlight through it. "Maybe I'm just a boy with different parts."

Leslie held back his next question, because something about Stevie's voice had gone dim, and said softly, "Maybe so."

Stevie skipped the purple stone over the surface of the stream. Cardinals chattered overhead, and a granddaddy long-legs traipsed over Leslie's forearm until he blew it loose with a puff. Their companionship nestled in the forest held a certain fragility; there was careful magic on the air, seeing as how no one else had stumbled upon them by chance or effort. Spar Creek and its horrors felt strangely distant.

"What's in the bag?" Stevie asked after another minute.

"Nothing much," he allowed, tapping his fingers on the satchel. "Some reading material, money the shopkeeper wouldn't let me spend."

"You're so bookish," he observed with brows raised, somewhere between charmed and confused. "What are you reading now?"

Flushing, he drew *De Profundis* from his bag and handed it over. Stevie passed the book from one hand to the other, never opening its covers, his eyes trained on Leslie's face instead. Eventually, he fumbled, "Well, you see, it's in part the journal of an Irishman writer who was jailed for an affair with a rich and cruel younger man, whose father disapproved of him."

"And do the boys who go for other boys get a special name, too?" Stevie asked.

His hazel-black eyes held a sudden intensity, almost ferocious in their regard. Leslie tensed against the pressure. The throb in his belly reminded him how long it had been since he last took a girl to bed. Mattingly was no girl, but he was handsome, and still naked to the waist. Leslie stalled answering for long enough that Stevie broke into a sly grin—guessing the effect he had.

"Then how long are you going to hang around on my behalf? You're risking your fool skin for nothing," he said.

"I'll stay until you're safe," he said, knowing he sounded melodramatic. "However I can help, just tell me."

Stevie huffed and said, "You sure like to feel important, huh? If you insist, then wait and see for yourself. I've got a plan, and I've been keeping a real good ear to the ground for what people are getting up to, whether they realize it or not." Sunlight caught the spit-shine as Stevie licked his chapped lips. "Now, why don't you read some of that book to me, before we head on back?"

Leslie narrated from the journal, stumbling mildly through the spicier portions, as their odd alliance—perhaps friendship—solidified with each word that dropped from his tongue to Stevie's ears. By the time he made his way back to the cabin, evening light stretched gold across the sky. Their stolen afternoon was a bubble, unpunctured by the unwanted pregnancy Leslie hadn't asked about, the specter of Floyd Marshall and the townsfolk turning their backs, or the amputated fingers and the broken house arrest. But as Leslie slunk back to the Hansall homestead, he realized he hadn't gotten an ounce of information about the boy's plot. *Played for a soft-hearted horny fool,* he chastised himself.

On the guest cabin porch sat Sarah Hansall, a familiar cardboard box on her lap.

Leslie stopped dead.

She rose imperiously from her chair and said, "Come on up here."

"Missus," he began.

"Don't *missus* me," she hissed, lifting the box. "After all you said to Pastor Holladay and the rest of us, you brought . . . things like this under my roof?"

"Those shouldn't have been forwarded here," Leslie said.

He mounted the stairs and reached for the box, but she snatched it behind her back. The diaphragms truly were not for the residents of Spar Creek, but that wouldn't matter to Sarah or anyone she'd told. Her stormy rage brooked no excuses.

"If you don't leave at first morning light," she said, low and mean, "I'll go to the council myself, and tell them you were pressing prophylactics on me and whoever else. See if they don't drag you behind a horse all the way to Hazard."

Leslie shook his head once, and said, "Please, ma'am. Couldn't you wait to blackmail me until the Jacobs girl delivers, or . . . at least until your husband comes back to escort me?"

"I don't need that man to tell me who can stay on *my* property," said Sarah.

"Fine," he agreed, stomach beneath the tread of his boots.

She skirted past him and rattled the box in warning.

"No more excuses. Tomorrow," she repeated.

Leslie almost wished she would've gloated, but she seemed fueled only by righteous anger. He hadn't warned her about the strange beast in the night; he hadn't gotten the Jacobs girl and her babies through safely; he hadn't convinced young Mattingly to saddle up behind him and head for Louisville. The work spread before him, unfinished, but the proverbial bell had rung the end of his time—unless he found some impossible compromise by dawn.

# XI.

Trouble arrived well before sunrise.

His precarious position kept Leslie's mind churning but his hands idle. Mattingly was confident in himself, but Leslie had buried many self-assured young men, and he couldn't help but worry—whether his concern was wanted or not. Sleep and solutions both escaped his grasp, while the threat of being hauled from bed and thrown out of town prevented him from stripping to the skivvies.

Which meant his boots were already laced when a hard four-beat knock jolted him. A man's voice called, "Miss Bruin, it's an emergency, are you there?"

He could hardly pretend otherwise. Switchblade tucked into his trouser pocket, he answered, "Getting presentable. What's happened, is it the Jacobs girl?"

"Hiram Collins has been shot," the man said.

"C'mon, nurse," barked a strained but recognizable Stevie.

*Lord, that boy is everywhere,* Leslie marveled, snatching his lamp and medical bag. Though he'd prepared for birthing, treating a gunshot wasn't that different.

On the porch stood two ghastly figures, sallow and spattered bloody. The sight of councilman Tim Landsdale beside outcast Stevie Mattingly gave Leslie another surprise, and judging by the pinched corners of his mouth, the man knew he'd given some secret away. Stevie, on the other hand, sported an expression as black and eager as coal slag over fire.

"Where is he?" Leslie asked.

"Out near the still," Stevie said.

"Show me."

The mismatched group entered the deer trails at a jog, dodging branches and leaping roots. Leslie stumbled several times but always regained his balance. The weighty satchel over his shoulder was a duty he meant to discharge; necessity kept him centered. At the trail split, the locals chose the path branch Leslie had yet to investigate.

"Where was he shot?" Leslie asked, clipped by breathlessness.

"Two rounds in the gut and one in the leg, from a revolver," answered Landsdale.

Stevie snarled, "He drew on that *motherfucker* Floyd, like an idiot."

He had a thousand questions, but first he asked, "So where's Floyd?"

"I took his gun and sent him home to deal with in the morning," the councilman said, grim. "The damage is already done."

Lantern light caught on Stevie's back muscles through his shirt, a bounding ripple that lashed the length of his spine—as if something shifted beneath. A blink dispelled the illusion, but the sense of strangeness clung on, the crooked shadow beneath the water.

The trail terminated at a gap among the trees. Leslie passed a moonshine still to crouch beside a ginger-haired young man whose belt had been tourniqueted around his upper thigh. He clutched a wadded jacket to his belly. Blood pooled on the ground, welled up from beneath his hands. His eyelids fluttered—unfortunately conscious.

"Cut some branches for a stretcher. Use your shirts and jackets," Leslie ordered.

The burst of fieldwork behind him pegged down his nerves. He opened his medic's satchel and gloved up before lifting Collins's quivering hands for a glimpse of the gut shots. What he saw made him grimace and press the makeshift bandage back down. Shifting toward the thigh, he sheared the trousers open and held the lamp close as he dared—relieved to find a furrowed graze rather than a lodged bullet.

"Sorry, Doc," Collins wheezed.

"Hush your mouth and hold your gut," Leslie said, kindly firm.

"Said he'd break her to the bit, even if he had to chain her to the house," he muttered. Glassy about the eyes, he watched Leslie rinse and disinfect the gouge. "Had to . . . show him what for."

"Respectable effort," he soothed.

"Stretcher's ready," Landsdale said.

"All right, fella." Leslie taped a bandage over the graze then grabbed Collins by the face to get him focused. "We're going to carry you back to town and send for a doctor. I'll do what I can in the meantime. Don't pass out, you hear me?"

"Yessir," he grunted.

Collins only stayed conscious until around the fording of the Spar.

The next two hours lurched by in fits. Tarp laid over the thin mattress in the cabin; lanterns scrounged from the barn and house; councilman Landsdale sent on the borrowed horse to summon the nearest real doctor; the missus Hansall hauling water to boil on the woodstove with wild eyes—and, ultimately, Stevie playing surgical assistant while Leslie did his absolute best to dig out the bullet that *hadn't* passed through. Collins remained insensate throughout.

No matter the care Leslie took cleaning the wounds, or suturing the blasted innards and flesh, he already knew the end: a bad gut shot without a proper hospital theater and surgeon and god's own luck was going to be fatal. Collins might survive the night, even another few days, but the odds of sepsis were staggering. Stevie had gone silent as the grave during triage, handing over tools and providing light as needed. He possessed the calm of someone who understood that a body was just so much meat—even a friend's body, harmed on his behalf.

Once the fog of surgery cleared and Leslie applied the last bandages around Collins's torso, he and Stevie stripped the bed, maneuvering fresh linens underneath him. He provided the man a healthy syringe of morphine to keep him from coming back too soon, and then stretched. His spine cracked from being hunched.

Stevie stood beside his dying friend.

"I'm going to kill him," he said, meditative.

Leslie had seen that slick, blank look on a hundred other faces. He said, "Come outside with me."

If he'd expected a fuss, Stevie surprised him once again by following without question. No lights showed at the main house. On the porch, lantern dangling from his left hand, Leslie heaved a breath. The cabin door thumped closed. Stevie waited behind him, unseen but felt. Weighing the risks of the night beast against those of being witnessed, he stepped into the yard. Around the backside of the cabin, no one could approach without their hearing. Hill-filtered moonlight lay soft across the forest and sheltered beneath the eaves.

Leslie wedged the lantern peg between cabin logs at eye level, planting his ass on the wall and fishing out his cigarettes. His fingers quivered as the adrenaline and agitation unspooled. Surgical gloves had kept his hands clean, but flecks of blood nonetheless dotted his forearms. Stevie silently posted up on the opposite side of the lamp. Leslie puffed one cig to life, pinched the filter between his fingers, and offered it to the boy. Stevie bent and caught it between his lips, one dry press against Leslie's fingertips—the same spot he brushed seconds later on his own mouth, lighting another cigarette. Tobacco smoke rooted him: tongue, gums, lungs, and nose accounted for. Their elbows bumped and neither moved aside, leaving their bones briefly at rest together.

Leslie asked, "Were you there, when they kicked off?"

"In a manner of speaking," Stevie said. Again, the low light reflected off his oil-slick eyes. "I'd made camp near the still, and I heard the boys working the batch, so I . . . thought I'd wait around. See if Floyd wandered into the woods for a real unlucky piss."

Leslie had been to war and back; the implications didn't trouble him any. Those years were behind him now, but he was the same person he'd always been: the person who had once lurked behind a row of latrines, waiting for a particular man to bluster into his trap. Severing someone's carotid was no challenge for a trained medic, and exacting his revenge for what had been done to him was as gratifying as he'd hoped. Stevie deserved the same satisfaction, if he so desired. Leslie crushed his finished cig beneath his boot, lit another, and offered a second to Stevie.

"I understand," he said.

Stevie exhaled. "You know the worst part? If you made me pick a man worth marrying, Hiram Collins would've done fine. He was a good friend. Could've caught me, maybe, excepting that he only likes girls. Now he's going to die for me instead."

Leslie refused to say *He could survive*. Platitudes served no purpose.

"Them fighting isn't your fault," he said instead.

Stevie took a long drag. The cherry threw orange glow onto his handsome face. After another minute, he confessed in a burst, "Floyd worked out a deal between his dad and ma and the preacher, that since he'd ridden me down like a goddamn horse, he could keep me. God cannot fathom what I am going to do to that man, soon as I get a chance."

"Or, you come with me, and we just leave them behind," Leslie said.

Stevie barked a laugh. "With Collins on his deathbed? No, I'm seeing things through."

"Sarah Hansall already has me in a bad spot," Leslie said. "She gave me 'til daybreak to get out of town. Waiting on the doctor might buy me time, but—"

"Trust me," Stevie interrupted.

Shadows danced around their feet, breeze tickling the lantern wick and its hot little flame. Leslie swallowed his frustration. He'd been a raw-blooded young thing once, and he understood the sweetness—the genuine security—of revenge. He even understood the desire to keep one's hometown, but the thing was, he *also* understood how dangerous Stevie's path of resistance would be. Sometimes survival meant ripping loose those domestic roots.

"What you said about Collins—being with a man wouldn't bother you, necessarily?" he asked, softer.

The facade of indifference cracked as Stevie's jaw flexed, cig bouncing between his lips. He muttered, "He made a good friend, whenever he forgot to treat me like a girl. And he was easy on the eyes."

"So, maybe, you're more of a boy who . . . goes for boys?" Leslie ventured.

"Fuck," Stevie grunted. He covered his eyes with his forearm, barring himself from seeing or being seen. "Fine, sure enough, but none of them are going to see it that way. Collins never could keep himself from calling me *miss* when he was trying to be fucking courtly."

The misery lacing Collins's name made Leslie's heart ache.

"I don't know, you're plenty handsome," he said. Stevie lowered his arm to glower, as if he thought them empty words. Under the eaves, with an eerie awareness of mortality hovering overhead, the tinder between them sparked. "In all seriousness, I've known my fair share of men who wouldn't be put off by your—business."

"Once it gets to fucking, it'll be all about the girl under the clothes again."

"What, you think boys don't get fucked?" Leslie said right back.

A blotchy flush dusted his cheekbones; he kept silent.

"Or, do you not know how?" he teased.

"What, is that something you learned from your books?" Stevie asked. He leaned closer, until their arms were pressed lengthwise and he had to tilt his chin down to meet Leslie's eyes. "Are you going to *teach* me?"

Hunger sprouted beneath the skin of Leslie's palms and within the smokey confines of his mouth. He said, low, "Brat."

Stevie grinned, teeth bared as much in challenge as invitation. Leslie flicked his guttering cigarette into the yard. The heartbeat-steady pulse between his legs was the height of foolishness.

"Didn't you just say you preferred men?" he asked.

"And you said you're partly one," Stevie replied. "An invert, ain't you?"

"Christ almighty," Leslie muttered to the stars above and hell below.

Now was not the time to explain the technicalities of the term.

"I suppose you and Collins are both after girls, though, huh," he muttered—and sidled *away*.

The separation of their skin wrenched at the pit of loneliness in Leslie's core. Mattingly was barely past his viciously bad experience—but didn't he still have the right to judge his own wants, and ask for them to be fulfilled? Seeing his posture tuck in from the perceived rejection, his knees and shoulder drawn by the gravity of embarrassment, was unbearable. Though he'd said it mockingly, Stevie was also correct that he'd read about a lot more ways to fuck than he'd personally experienced. Leslie had been shown the ropes on the proper ways to pursue girls in Paris, but he'd fooled around before, and had witnessed his share of soldier boys on each other. With all those combined, surely he could extrapolate.

"Never said I *wouldn't* go to bed with someone manlier," he murmured. "I was stationed on the front, you know."

Stevie hesitated. His bluster had washed away, an anxious tension left in its wake—recalling the hurts that had brought them together.

"Really?" he murmured, the single word plush and clingy as kneaded dough.

"You just have to tell me how you need it," Leslie said.

The flinch that rocked his body might've come from arousal, or fear, or humiliation. Leslie hadn't spent enough time figuring out the boy and his wants to know for certain. Careful, he plucked at Mattingly's belt loop to reel him near, cataloging his red face and avoidant eyes. Unearthing the smoldering space where their particular desires merged was the trickiest part; luckily, though, servicing his partners always gave Leslie the right kind of thrill.

"I've got to know what not to do," he said. "Since I don't want to hurt you."

The determination Leslie had come to expect from Stevie creased his brow—before he closed the distance and planted his feet between Leslie's. Chest pressed against chest, belly to belly, he muttered almost against Leslie's mouth: "Do whatever a man would, if I were his boy."

"Stop me if you need," he said.

Their mouths landed crooked; their noses mashed together. Stevie had chapped lips. Leslie got one hand around his jaw and the other on his neck, angling him correct with firm fingers that made him gasp. Stevie craned his neck downward, shoving himself closer on instinct as he tried to shrink to fit within his smaller partner's embrace. His grasp on Leslie's waist clenched spasmodically tight.

Leslie reared back and hissed, "Calm down, boy. You'll get what you want."

Stevie stopped dead with his wet mouth wide and a hazy expression. *There it is,* Leslie thought. A flare of arousal reminded him of the sorts of things he no longer allowed girls to do unto his body—things he still touched himself to, safe and alone. He had a fairly good guess about how to treat such a needful creature: conscientious, but far from kind. With a deft twist, he ducked outside their embrace.

"Face the wall," he said.

"What?" Stevie floundered, half-turned toward him.

"I said, face the wall," Leslie ordered.

The boy gave him a soulful, confused stare with eager hands afloat. Leslie stepped close, grabbed the back of his neck and a handful of firm ass cheek, and turned him. When he resisted on instinct Leslie leaned heavy on his back. The firm handling astonished a moan out of Stevie; finally, he shuffled full-length flat against the wall. Without needing to be told, he lifted both hands onto the logs overhead. Leslie noted his stronger response to physical guidance, as opposed to spoken orders, and jerked Mattingly's trouser buttons loose. Though he felt charged and alight with desire, he was aware of the need for quickness: the possibility of being caught in flagrante delicto, the dying man on the other side of the wall, the mismatched experience that made him responsible for Stevie's pleasure. He rucked the trousers and underwear to Stevie's knees, then stomped them down around his ankles.

Moonlight and oil glow highlighted the peachy roundness of the boy's buttocks. Stevie was already panting for breath, his fingers wedged between the cabin logs. Leslie ran the blade of his palm between the cheeks, massaging his crack and asshole. Though he aimed no farther down, a dab of wetness smeared the knuckles of his index finger. He'd fucked this sort of hole before; he hadn't lied about his *practice*. Stevie wriggled and arched against his concentrated rubbing as if he weren't sure where to move, or how to do it right, only seeking more sensation.

"Sir," he groaned.

Leslie surged forward to bite the nape of his neck, crushing his own hand between them; *sir,* colored with such trust, made him desperate for flesh between his teeth. Stevie yelped, higher and louder than the crickets and rustling water. Leslie slapped the other palm over his mouth and got a tongue wedged between his fingers for the trouble.

"You can't be noisy," he hissed.

Stevie nodded jerkily and attempted to suck on his palm.

*Jesus Christ,* he almost moaned, a straight line pulsing between the clumsy damp suction and his groin. The trousers around his ankles prevented Stevie from spreading his legs farther, but he certainly tried while Leslie jammed two salt-slick fingers down his own throat—prompting the thickest, slimiest drool he could manage on short notice. Stevie had asked to be his boy, and Leslie would fuck him the way he wanted, even if that meant avoiding more readily available lubrication. Surprise got the entire first finger into Stevie's hole before he clamped around the intrusion with a strangled yelp. However, the eager and clumsy backward push of his hips overrode the near-hurt noises. Leslie circled his palm, stimulating the clinging rim, and at the next slight give tucked another finger inside. The molten softness of Mattingly's guts clutched and released, clutched and released, to the pattern of his heaving breath.

Leslie angled his hand downward, curved his fingers, massaged a firm circle. Beneath his other hand he felt Stevie's mouth drop loose and open. Perhaps later, if a later came, he'd guide that sloppy tongue down between his legs.

"Easy there," Leslie whispered against his shoulder. "If we were at my boardinghouse, I'd have a cock for you, but you'll need to make do with this tonight."

"Mmn—" The word was meaningless, garbled.

For safety's sake, he lifted the restraining hand. "What's that?"

"Please, more," Stevie gasped.

Leslie gave him *more,* until his biceps and forearm burned. He gnawed, and tongued, and sucked a low collar of bruises around Stevie's neck from behind; their continually shifting bodies aligned such that his clothed crotch pressed to the bony rise of Stevie's hip, each bump prompting a shot of pleasure. Once friction started to drag on his fingers he withdrew them, spat fresh on the hole as well as his hand, and forced in deeper. Stevie flailed and sobbed and snagged a fistful of hair at the crown of Leslie's head. The yank on his roots almost made him shout.

"Finish yourself, go on," he said.

"I—don't—" Stevie panted.

"Your cock," he snarled, "rub it 'til you come."

Less than a minute after, the muscles of Stevie's hole pulsed with a struck-silent orgasm. Leslie rested his forehead on the boy's shoulder, slowing his pace by degrees to ease the climax to its conclusion—while managing his ferocious urge to continue for however long his boy could handle. Once the squeezing calmed, he felt safe to remove his fingers. The withdrawal pulled another wheezy sob from Stevie. Moths floated around their bent heads, bumping the glass case of the lantern: safe from the fire inside, but aiming for it all the same. Leslie turned him around and gathered him into an embrace. Tears soaked the collar of his shirt, but given the way Stevie hid his face and clung, it was probably best to let the crying pass unacknowledged. He combed the fingers of his clean hand through the sex-loosened mass of Stevie's hair, blood singing with the satisfaction of a job well done.

"Hush now, good boy, it's all right," he whispered.

# XII.

The sky had begun to swallow stars down its gullet by the time Stevie roused, tucked under Leslie's arm on the cabin floor. He'd held vigil over the morphine-addled Collins and the boy curled into a comma against his side. In their underclothes, laid on top of their trousers and shirts, the technical sameness of their bodies was remarkable to Leslie—though each interpreted the shape of their flesh through a different lens, one an invert and the other a young man. Stevie pressed his nose into Leslie's armpit with a groan and threw an arm across his breasts. Dawn sifted over their embrace like finely powdered sugar.

"We could go now, before anyone else wakes up," Leslie whispered.

Stevie shifted an inch and bit the meat of Leslie's tit through his cotton undershirt. He flinched, though his nipples stiffened visibly. The boy rubbed bony fingers between the slats of his ribs. The exploration felt partly erotic, partly curious: testing the boundaries of what was allowed. Leslie wondered if he'd ever really *touched* someone before, unhurried, and sighed through his nostrils.

Stevie released his bite, mumbling, "Would this be how it is for me in the city, like you keep talking about?"

"Maybe so, if it's what you choose," Leslie said. "But however things would be it's better than goddamn Spar Creek. Neither of us is safe here anymore."

"I can't go," he replied. "Not before I get mine back."

Leslie remembered the terrible attention of the crowd, no one willing to speak a word in Stevie's defense, as well as Sarah Hansall's ultimatum. He asked, "Is it worth your life?"

Stevie propped himself on one elbow. His other hand on Leslie's ribs was grounding and suffocating—sticky, glued together. Leslie couldn't parse the emotions on his face, their peaks and valleys foreign to him after such little time as companions. A single fuck, resonate though their bodies might afterward, was no replacement for weeks of conversation.

"Do you always run, when playing polite stops working?"

Leslie hadn't braced himself for that question. *No,* a leashed and buried element of him whispered; *Yes,* cried the greater portion, dedicated to his survival and nothing else.

"Sometimes," Stevie murmured, kneading the plump swell of Leslie's stomach, "isn't it better to be the monster they already think you are?"

"Stevie."

Two soft thumps on his belly. "Give me another day or two."

"I don't know that I've got a day or two left in this town," Leslie replied, rudderless.

Stevie pressed their foreheads together. Tender though blunt, he said, "We fucked; that doesn't make me your charge. I ain't done here yet. If you need to leave, then go, but I'll finish my business."

Leslie smothered his sore, wanting spirit back down. His nose bumped the freckles on Stevie's cheek. What comprised his duty, for the FNS and for Spar Creek, for himself and for Stevie, he was unsure—but he couldn't leave a man behind enemy lines, and neither could he toss the boy over the back of his horse. *What about me, aren't you worried at all,* he thought.

Aloud, he said, "Stubborn."

"Never claimed otherwise."

Stevie smacked a kiss on his mouth then heaved himself to standing. He dressed in the dull glow before sunrise, and Leslie examined the musculature he'd groped: dense abdominals, rock-solid calves, and firm, round buttocks. Seeing the person who stood before him as a man was simple enough; reconciling the warmth that kindled with the clear and coherent self-definition he'd spent years crafting was . . . less so. He'd exaggerated slightly while building their sex. In truth, like the man lying insensate on the other side of the cabin, he mostly had experience with girls. He had as much to learn as he had to teach. If only he could phone Addie; she'd seen it all before, and might have the words to set him right.

Stevie leaned against the window frame, tugging his boots on.

Leslie asked, "What are you planning to do?"

The smile he got in return was a toothy slash.

"Hopefully, some damage," he said, and leapt out the window.

Leslie scrambled onto his knees to watch Stevie's retreat. The cadence of his jog was feline, loose, and strange—as if he *melted* toward the trees, his edges gone liquid. Leslie hadn't asked about the stubbed, absent fingers, or what those had to do with the witch cave, the mutilated deer, and the night beast haunting his cabin. There was a sense of honor around the silence; the same honor his fellow nurses had given him when he'd returned to the surgical tent washed in blood with a straight razor to dispose of. Observing the Mattingly boy made some slumbering thing inside him remember, and begin to yearn. He'd been the monster, once.

Left alone with Collins's labored breathing, however, his trepidation increased. Whatever had been summoned by the secret violence of Spar Creek, he prayed it would catch the right people and spare the rest. After he'd washed, dressed, and gloved up to check the man's wounds, the expected knock came. On the other side of the door stood Tim Landsdale, another man with a doctor's bag, and an older woman bearing a terrible grief Leslie assumed must be the matron Collins.

"Come on in," he said.

"What's been done?" the doctor asked.

Tim held the woman by the shoulders, providing restraint and comfort, while Leslie reported his treatment. He attempted delicacy but nonetheless had to confirm, "The internal damage was serious, sir." He heard the man's mother grunt.

"Thank you," the doctor said. "You all should wait outside."

On the porch, Missus Collins glared across the yard and said, "They let the Marshall boy run amok, and this is what he does to my son. For the sake of some dishonorable girl."

"Be calm now, Jane. Miss Bruin here did her best, and the doctor will too," Landsdale said.

"All this trouble started when she came here," the woman said, turning her eyes on Leslie. "Encouraging such deplorable behavior, don't think we don't know—a degenerate, just like Pastor Holladay warned us."

*I spent the night sewing your fool son's innards back together,* he did not respond.

Tim Landsdale sighed but spoke no defense. At the main house, Sarah Hansall waited in the back doorway. Squatting in town any longer was asking for trouble, and though he still doubted anyone would murder him outright, death wasn't the worst thing these people might do. Stevie could attest to that. Fear coated his mouth. Jackson Hansall appeared behind his wife, to Leslie's surprise, only to step around her and gesture for Leslie as he strode off toward the barns.

The horse Hansall had ridden back to town was hitched to the center rail, ready to be curried. Her ears swiveled to follow Leslie and Jackson through the barn, away from prying eyes. The grimace on his face boded poorly. Near the unused stall at the back, Hansall slipped an envelope from his trouser pocket and handed it over. The sender was the Frontier Nursing Service and it had been addressed to Leslie, but the seal was already torn. Leslie flicked a questioning glance at the man. He looked like he'd bitten into a rotten apple.

Below the official letterhead, Leslie read: *It has come to our attention that you accepted receipt of a package being tracked by the postmaster general, which contained obscene materials procured by yourself. As these materials are in direct dispute with the mission and beliefs of the Frontier Nursing Service, we regret to inform you that you have been terminated from your position effective immediately*... The rest of the letter carried logistical particulars: receipt of his final paycheck, instructions to return official materials to the nearest appropriate hospital upon leaving Spar Creek.

There went his remaining leg to stand on. Relief, rage, and anxiety balled together like snakes inside him. If only Stevie had been willing to go, or the managers had waited another fortnight—

"You've gone and put me in a poor position, army girl," said Hansall as Leslie neatly refolded the notice. "Came back this morning to Sarah bellowing at me that we need to haul you out of town, that you had to put Collins up in the cabin after he got shot in a duel, and that you'd been secretly keeping—well, you know what they were."

"I doubt it matters, but that situation isn't quite what it looks like," he said.

Hansall smiled his usual gregarious smile, but nevertheless

shrugged a refusal. If even the man who'd supported him thus far couldn't abide his presence another few days, he had no option left. The hitched horse whinnied at them, tired of being ignored.

Hansall said, "You understand it's nothing personal, but . . . I have to ask you to get on your way. Whether or not I'm in agreement doesn't matter much when people get to feeling a way about things."

Stevie was still out there, up to who knew what, and Leslie had to make one last attempt. He said, "What about Hiram Collins? If I hadn't been here last night, that boy would be dead in the woods, and instead he made it until the doctor arrived. Does that carry no weight?"

"Not when folks blame your presence for Mattingly acting out, and thereby for the duel," Hansall replied. He rubbed a nostril with his thumb, performing *aw shucks*. "Miss, I've seen my fair share of Europeans. I know they do things different. But we don't. No one here abides that kind of—licentiousness. Honest, it's for your own good, getting away from Spar Creek. You've already done your part."

"Could you bargain for me, get me one more day?" he asked.

"I don't believe so," Hansall said, implying *and wouldn't even if I could.*

Leslie nodded jerkily. "Once the doctor finishes with Collins, I'll pack my things," he said.

Severance letter crumpled in his fist, he turned from Hansall—but paused when the man cleared his throat. Charged tension hung. Finally, he said, "When I rode in, everyone was carrying on about some big, ugly beast coming from the woods to menace the Marshalls. Slashed up their livestock, plus some others' besides. Saying it was a hill devil. I don't think you should be in Spar Creek when they decide it ain't a panther, but a witch. You gather?"

Understanding dribbled down Leslie's backbone. If he abandoned Stevie to his plot, and the townsfolk caught hold of him, what might happen did not bear imagining. Leslie didn't wish to spend the rest of his days wondering, but never learning, what had become of the boy.

"Goddamnit, but I surely do," he muttered, to himself as much as to Hansall.

Sarah Hansall posted herself on the porch to watch Leslie pack his service saddlebags. The Collins family, with the assistance of a neighbor's cart, had shifted a feverish, nonresponsive Hiram back beneath the roof he'd been birthed under—never speaking aloud that they awaited the inevitable. Though he'd clapped Leslie on the shoulder for his efforts, the county doctor had seemed eager to escape from oppressive Spar Creek as well. Forced out under politely militant watch, Leslie's best bet would be stopping somewhere outside the township to await Mattingly. He'd have to leave the boy a message, perhaps with Auntie Marge. It was obvious, however, that no one intended to let him out of their sight long enough to do so. He wouldn't be surprised if the pastor himself decided to ride behind him all the way to Hazard.

The thought made him snort, hands packing diligent but slow.

"What, are you so proud of yourself?" Sarah said nastily.

Leslie lifted his chin and glared. Without his careful, friendly mask papered over it, the cold truth of how much hate he stored for people like her showed through. She recoiled on instinct and grasped at her cross. Leslie sneered, the most honest expression he'd allowed himself for months outside of being buried to the palm inside Stevie's guts. He had no reason to continue pretending, and maybe if she got a bad enough shock, she'd run off, leaving him a minute to plan.

With great relish, he said, "Shouldn't I be asking you that, you godbothering bitch?"

Sarah went milk-foam white then bright red under her freckles. Her lips popped open like she'd been slapped. Leslie hooked thumbs through his belt loops and rocked back on his heels, grinning. He had just taken a breath to continue dressing Sarah down when someone shrieking "Nurse!" over a horse's gallop cut him short, and instead he elbowed past her to vault down the porch steps. Young Mister Jacobs reined his horse to a sweat-frothed stop in the yard.

Of course there could be no good news in Spar Creek.

"What's happened?" Leslie barked.

"The babies are coming, and she's hurt bad," he said.

Even the righteous Missus Hansall stepped aside when he thundered up the steps to grab his medical bag—only to remember he hadn't refilled it after the emergency the night before. Spitting profanities bluer than the sky, he stuffed the bag with fresh gloves and all the surgical sundries in reach. Sarah hovered, her hands clasped before her, a complicated frown on her face.

Leslie leaned close and hissed, "If she dies, it's on your heads, every last one of you."

He leapt up astride the horse behind the Jacobs boy, who wrangled it competently despite his obvious terror. "Did they send for me?" he asked.

"No, but I'm the one who married her," he said.

"Fuck," he muttered.

Leslie interrogated Jacobs as they rode, his voice smoothed calm to keep the young man from panicking worse. He learned nothing comforting. Beth's granny and an aunt had caught the first infant, but its passing had wounded her sorely; they'd been using hog grease on their hands as they'd always done, thereby increasing her risk of infection; the second babe was stuck, and the young man hadn't the knowledge to explain how.

Screams ricocheted through the trees around the Jacobs homestead.

Leslie packed away the emotions that could distract him from his work, horror chief among them. His duty was owed to the girl; the rest of them could go hang. Jacobs swung himself from the horse and left the animal unhitched, sprinting through the open door with Leslie close behind. What he saw on the bed at the center of the room gave him the strength to gesture the aunties away, with enough force that no one dared argue. Training possessed him so triage logic could pilot his body—and he labored, as best he could with the supplies on hand, for as long as it took.

But he'd known as soon as he came inside how little he'd be able to help.

# XIII.

Another hour passed before the father held both babies to his chest, their squalls quieted to snuffling. Leslie scrubbed clean at the basin, vacant-eyed, next to the house matron who had begun to cry. The now-grandfather was caring for the body of the girl who had been their child. Their grief flowed around Leslie, and awfulness bubbled within him. He'd never lost a birthing mother before. As with Hiram Collins, so with Beth Jacobs: utterly preventable. *You should've called for me,* he wouldn't say.

As he gathered unused supplies, the auntie bundling ruined sheets hissed, "If she hadn't been carted all over town, maybe this wouldn't have happened."

Her face held nothing but pain and rage. They'd already forgotten how he saved the second baby. Exhausted, he abandoned his remaining materials where they sat, swung the satchel over his shoulder, and walked out unhindered. Beside the main road, he crouched and bellowed into clenched fists. The creases of his knuckles carried a faint charnel-house stink. The urge to savage his flesh with his teeth flared, dissipated.

Though Spar Creek was finished with him, he wasn't finished with it, and in the wake of tragedy its eyes had left him. Afraid of being discovered, Leslie crossed to the opposite side of the lane and broke through the underbrush. He set off in what he believed to be the direction of Marge's homestead. The Jacobs family were near enough to her property, and the woods would spare him from strangers' sight—though forging a trail doubled the time the road would've taken. Marge's empty yard gave him pause when he arrived, wary of capture. He crouched in the bushes with forearms draped over his knees. Breeze rustled cropped grass; glass windchimes tinkled. Buckets of sweat seeped from his pores.

Having eventually waited long enough to soothe his nerves, he crept through the garden. A note was pinned to the screen door: *Gone to visit with relatives four–five days.* Leslie thumped his fist against the doorframe. Beneath the house an animal rumbled warningly; he stepped back quick, and one of the orange cats emerged with ears pinned.

"Settle down," he murmured, edging away.

Once he'd opened a gap between them the cat merely bristled, protective. Leslie knew how to take a hint. Apparently, so did the auntie. He had to assume that she'd beaten a strategic retreat before the superstitious rage turned on her house of herbs, before she drew fire for tending to wayward boy-girls. She'd left Leslie and Stevie alone to face the rising tide. Maybe she'd offered Stevie the same advice he had: *Get out, before it costs you more than you have to lose.* There was nothing quite so blinding as furious youth. Leslie returned to the deer trails, dread knotting his guts.

He paused on the banks of the Spar. The hidden path he'd followed to the witch cave was undisturbed, but that meant little when it came to a woodsman of Mattingly's caliber. Leslie had no lantern or camping pack, but also no hope of begging another night off the Hansalls.

"Stevie," he called. "Hey, brat—Mister Mattingly—you out here?"

Only the creek and the birds chattered back.

"Stevie!" he shouted.

The echo rang his eardrums. Whether the boy was within

hearing or not, the sense of exposure drove Leslie farther down the path. He didn't want to meet a stranger on the trail. He emerged onto the Hansall homestead as the evening gloom painted hollows under buildings. Supper lights glowed in the main house. Through the back windows, Leslie saw Sarah bustling around the kitchen. He rounded the front, past the sleepy hound dog, to knock one last time. Jackson answered after a moment's pause, leaning against the doorframe such that his shadow swallowed Leslie. The man tilted his chin. Wrinkles pinched his brow like tanned dough.

"The babies were both delivered safe, but . . ." Leslie trailed off with a shake of the head.

"Mighty sorry to hear that," Jackson said.

Behind him, on the living room floor, his children played jacks. The rubber ball bounced with a thump, but the girl was so busy spying on her father's conversation that she missed her first grab. Catching Leslie's eye, she paled and turned away.

"I've lost, or as good as lost, two patients in twenty-four hours, Mister Hansall," he said, allowing himself to sound desperate. "Just grant me one night to rest, and I swear I'll be gone by sunrise."

Firelight danced over the crags of his face, lending depth to his frown. Hansall glanced toward the kitchen door, sighed from the chest, and nodded.

"One night more, Nurse, but then you've really got to go," he said.

"Thank you kindly," Leslie replied. He didn't need to fake his relief.

Crossing the darkening yard toward the cabin he felt as if he'd given the chamber of a revolver another spin before pressing the barrel against his temple. The forest lurked, threatening to swallow him down. Leslie barred the door between himself and the world, then took stock of his possessions. Marge had told him to be ready for swift action, but she herself had only been swift in flight: what a piss-poor omen.

Nightfall arrived with the croaking of frogs. Leslie lay stiff as a corpse, hands resting on his belly, dressed except for his boots. Saddlebags waited by the door with his satchel on top. The rifle and quilt had been removed while he was gone, and a splotch of rust-brown blood dotted the bottom corner of the bedsheet where the rubber had failed to protect it. His stuffy cabin echoed with water-whispers, and past its walls some felid beast stalked; past the Hansall property line waited Mattingly, whose sacrifice had crafted, or summoned, or unleashed the thing—Leslie couldn't be sure. He'd spent the better portion of his life brushing past the teeth of monsters, human or otherwise, but he still felt unprepared.

For so long he'd drifted from one duty to another, guided by rules and orders, severed from his own desire. That had ended with Spar Creek and its horrors, its temptations. The untimely deaths he'd overseen left grave mist on his cheeks. If he hadn't tied himself to Mattingly, committed to the boy's future, he'd've saddled a horse and been gone in the dark.

Some time later, a steady rap sounded on the door.

Sarah said, "Are you there?"

Leslie groaned and rose to unbar the door, prepared for another argument.

Through the crack he glimpsed Ames Holladay, and a flock of bobbing lights behind him. Leslie flung his shoulder against the door, but he was too light and too late, as the pastor forced it open by boot. Leslie stumbled against the bedframe, rattling the brass feet against the boards; the Missus Hansall and a stranger fell onto him, grabbing a wrist in each hand. His unclad heel flailed into Sarah's kneecap and buckled her. Her grip slipped; he wrenched loose and grabbed for the switchblade in his opposite pocket while the stranger fought to control his dominant wrist.

The preacher struck him hard across the face.

Bell rung, Leslie went limp, and by the time the splotches cleared from his eyes he'd been wrestled still. The stranger's arm cuffed him beneath the jaw, forcing his teeth together. On the porch, a mixed-gender gaggle of folks stared wide as owls—including the blond brothers he'd met the first night in town. Though Jackson wasn't among their number, the closed door at the main house implied he wasn't coming to stop them either.

"I wrote letters. People know where I am," Leslie wheezed.

Holladay raised one patrician eyebrow and smiled. "You speak like I'm not a man of God, miss. Are you so frightened of the Lord's grace?"

Sarah dumped the box of contraceptives on the floor and pointed to his bags. The pastor neatly plucked up the travel satchel. Leslie rose on tiptoe to sip air through his compressed throat, woozy. The window was his only path of escape from the cabin. He had no good options, but once the posse carried him outside, there would be plenty more bad ones.

"Your reading material is as degenerate as I expected," Holladay said as he unearthed novel after novel. His expression of disgust told Leslie he either recognized them for what they were, or simply assumed as much. "Did you believe the people of Spar Creek too stupid to read? To know what sort of perversion and filth you'd brought with you, right under our noses?"

The chokehold loosened marginally when he stopped struggling, along with the grip crushing his wrists together atop his breasts. He said, hoarse, "I've done nothing wrong."

"You led our confused lamb astray, and now she has plied her troth with devils. A man has been shot, a mother has died. A demon hunts among us. We will deal with those troubles in time, but you . . . you are the first." Passion glowed behind his eyes. To Leslie's captor, he said, "Bring her along to the creek. Mister Marshall, grab her ankles, or she'll get loose."

Knowledge clicked into place like a padlock's chambers when one of the blond pair stepped forward, grinning nastily. Floyd Marshall, whom Leslie hadn't managed to lay eyes on despite hearing his name bandied all around, had come to dole out another punishment.

The seconds between the chokehold loosening and the man bear-hugging Leslie around his upper arms to haul him off the ground instead wasn't long enough. Leslie fought, but Marshall caught his flailing legs, forcing them together at the knees and ankles while Sarah gathered the books and letters from atop the mattress. The presence of two women in the processional gave him hope he wouldn't be raped; he was less confident he wouldn't be murdered. Leslie stopped struggling as the townsfolk carted his limp body between them toward the woods, aiming to conserve a burst of energy for the right moment.

"What's your plan, pastor?" he called out.

"A baptism, to cleanse your degenerate spirit," Holladay said.

*He's going to drown me,* Leslie realized with a lurch.

The woods devoured them, blackness on all sides barely punctured by bobbing lanterns. Sarah Hansall strode along beside the crumpled, captive Leslie like the handmaiden at a wedding: chin held aloft, arms full of paper instead of flowers. Leslie's neck was bent at an awkward angle, the first man's chest jolting his head forward with each step. His thumbs and pinkies tingled, and he couldn't reach his knife.

The creek babbled loud, then louder still, through an otherwise silent forest. At its banks, the men abruptly released Leslie. He dropped on his back hard enough to knock the wind from him, rocks stabbing through his shirt. He flopped onto his belly, a single knee drawn up to sprint, but someone's foot stamped him down. The pressure increased as he tried to crawl, popping his spine and crushing the last air from his chest. The chunk of fluorspar living in his shirt pocket bit the meat of his breast.

"Witness here tonight an act of consecration," the preacher said from above. "We will wash clean this sinner, who dies and lives again as did the Lord Jesus, emerging newborn from the waters."

Leslie stuffed his hand into his pocket and grasped the switchblade handle. Mud smeared his face. The woman whose name he did not know sang one wavering verse of a hymn: "Have you been to Jesus for the cleansing power, are you washed in the blood of the Lamb?" The others joined, their ghastly chorus echoing, "Are you fully trusting in His grace this hour, are you washed in the blood of the Lamb?" Hands grasped Leslie by the shoulders, arms, and legs. He tried to bite, but their jackets deflected his teeth, and when the glint of his knife flashed one of the men batted it from his grasp.

The pastor sloshed into the creek accompanied by their wail: *Are you washed in the blood?* Leslie spat cusses and scrapped for all he was worth, but the crowd easily threw him into the stream face first. Rocks cut his palms, lashed his forehead. He rose sputtering onto all fours. Someone grabbed a fistful of his hair and hauled him over backward, bloody water streaming into his eyes, then dunked him beneath the surface again.

Water roared in his ears as air escaped from his traitor lungs. He grabbed the pastor's elbow with both hands and wrenched his arm to the side, crunching upward to steal one gasp above the current. ". . . and of the Holy Ghost," he heard clear as day, over the blasting of his heartbeat in his skull.

An open hand slammed down over his face and forced him beneath the Spar once more. Pain exploded from his nose, his scalp, and the rupture of his cheek against his teeth. Water rushed down his esophagus; the reflexive cough drew another lungful of creek silt. Leslie thrashed, his bare heels skidding through mud. Holladay's fingers dug furrows into his forehead. Desperate, he clawed the pastor's wrists and hands, gouging his flesh but unable to budge him.

Then the pastor's steady grip abruptly faltered, and disappeared.

Leslie reared from the water, kicking away toward the opposite bank on instinct and hacking up what he'd inhaled. A terrified shriek echoed through the clearing; somehow, it wasn't his own. Shock frosted his thoughts, sweet and poisonous and impossible to reason through, but no one tried to drag him back into the Spar. He rolled onto his side to discover why he'd been released, and saw the church mob scrabbling away through the trees in all directions. His waterlogged ears muffled their screaming and hollering.

On the stream bank crouched the beast that stalked the night, its eyes only for Leslie even as a wealth of other prey scattered. None of those congregants had paused, either to rescue their fellows or to stand and fight; they fled at the sight alone. Besides the pinkness of its mouth and throat glimpsed between razor teeth made of fluorspar, the creature was dark as pitch: coal and ash given life. A membranous covering lay over its lambent, striking yellow eyes. It resembled both a panther and a man on all fours, though its shape seemed to ooze against the woods beyond. Leslie had trouble saying if its glittering fangs rose from a mouth, or a muzzle. It planted one clawed, thumb-jointed hand into the flow of the Spar.

A pathetic, instinctive whine escaped Leslie.

It paused. The head tipped one direction then another as ash sifted through the air. Muscles and tendons worked beneath its slick skin, neither fur nor flesh. The remaining lantern, dropped on its side, guttered out. Limned by starlight falling through the canopy above, Leslie watched the creature recede *into* itself.

The flowing Spar sounded like laughter.

Stevie Mattingly stood where the beast had been crouched, stark naked, his fingers tipped in scything claws. Blackness clung in patches around his wrists, ankles, and groin. His human teeth glared eerie white, and his eyes still held a glow. He crossed the creek in two steps and dropped to kneel astride Leslie. The last remnants of coal and claw dissolved, leaving behind a boy who tenderly cupped Leslie's bloodied face.

"Do you see?" he whispered, fierce as a forest god. "I had to get the hang of what it made me, first, but now I'm more than any of them could have imagined."

He slanted their mouths together for a devouring kiss; the taste of his spit was loam and copper. No wonder the creature had been circling Leslie's cabin. Dumbstruck and near-drowned, Leslie said past Stevie's ardently clumsy teeth, "Fuck, you're stunning."

# XIV.

Sopping clothes sucked against his skin. Stevie, startlingly nude, inspected his shallow wounds and thumped his back to force up another wretched tablespoon of water. His books and letters scattered the length of the creek, disintegrating under its wet kiss. *You're safe and you've found him, now get on a horse and go,* Leslie thought. When Stevie crouched before him, knees spread wide, even world-wise Leslie jerked his gaze up from its natural resting point. The boy's human form moved with the same liquid grace as his monstrous one—or maybe that self-possession had always been there, and the forest had simply built on it. As teeth-chattering adrenaline dissipated, what rose from beneath was the cleanest fury Leslie had experienced in a decade.

Stevie asked, "Are you going to be all right?"

Leslie rotated his wrists and ankles, cracked his sore neck. His joints seemed fine, though breathing hurt his ribs. The surface wounds were scratches. Stevie observed the testing motions.

"It does seem so," Leslie replied.

Silently they measured one another, until Leslie turned and stuck his bloodied feet into the creek. Its cool tongue soothed the sting. The watchful woods, unsettling before, now felt welcoming—maybe pleased that he'd fucked their favored creature right-good.

Stevie said, "I've been keeping an eye on things from outside of town, waiting for a good moment. I heard Holladay calling folks together for a night sermon about the problem of *me.* I hadn't expected they would come after you first, 'til I headed 'round to get you and saw the cabin all messed up—so, I'm sorry. Glad I could scare the fuckers off, but . . . well, I figure that's where they're running back to."

Spar Creek's current floated the waterlogged remains of one of his letters past his feet.

"I am," he said with deliberation, "very, *very* angry."

Stevie knelt with elbows planted on Leslie's shoulders and hands dangling loose over his chest. Leslie loosely interlaced their fingers. The charge caught between their skin quickened his breath; he nudged his head backward against Stevie's chest. Fire, lightning, the bell toll or the red string: every metaphor for connection he'd ever read, all the dead-end fantasies he'd crafted for himself, paled in comparison to the simple rightness he felt holding his boy's hand. After the war ended, he'd tried to shape himself into a softer person. He'd tried to model his novels, his mentors, to make room for a good love, but the relationships he'd attempted and *how* he'd attempted them were never going to fit his truth.

Blunt teeth pinched the shell of his ear. Stevie, whose hand was as rough from labor as Leslie's own, squeezed his fingers.

"And what do you want to do about that?" he asked, before flicking his tongue across the notch connecting jaw and neck.

*Fast learner.* Leslie replied, "Do you have a plan?"

"I gather you prefer to be in charge, but if you trust me to lead," he said, "why don't we do some *hunting*?"

Knifing arousal spoke straight through his mouth: "Never said I *had* to be in charge."

"And you ain't squeamish, either, are you," Stevie rumbled, eager because he already knew the answer.

"No," he said.

"Then we better be quick, before I lose his smell," Stevie said. "Give me just a second."

He flitted into the surrounding trees, the white slash of his body melting into their darkness, but returned almost instantaneously with a bundle of clothes and boots dangling from his hand by the laces. He must've developed the habit of stripping quick before he shifted shapes. The boots he tossed to Leslie; the loose trousers and shirt he yanked back on as he said, "Wear these, I'm fine without."

Leslie stuffed his lacerated feet inside. The fit was too loose, but after he drew the laces, they'd serve. He'd dealt with borrowed boots full of trench mud—anything else was an improvement. Stevie lifted his chin and inhaled deeply, almost huffing.

"Fool ran off by himself, and in the wrong direction," he murmured.

When he gestured *come along*, Leslie snagged fingers through his belt loop to follow blindly into the woods. The easy, dexterous confidence with which Stevie led showed how much time he'd spent skulking around Spar Creek in his other form.

Before the moment escaped him, or their prey neared, Leslie asked, "The monster, the transformation: what . . . did that cost you?"

"It doesn't seem fair to call it a cost," Stevie said. He darted a glance over his shoulder, barely visible to only-human Leslie. "Remember, I was born right on this ground. These woods, their land, knew me already; it was ready to make a fair trade. Eat some of it, let it eat some of me, you know? The real *blood of my blood*."

"But your fingers," he balked.

Stevie snorted. "Weird as hell: the cuts didn't hurt and healed clean, straightaway. Aunt Marge told me where the cave was, said people had kept altars there for as long as there'd been people. Once I crawled down in there, I just knew what to do."

Leslie remembered his dreams, the sultry hills enfolding him; he realized he had sensed its safety, its *willingness*, but hadn't known what was being offered. "And that fixed the . . . ?"

"The first time I shifted back I felt all my insides rearranging—like, I had control of them. So I made myself bleed again, no fuss, no trouble," Stevie replied.

Relief swept through Leslie. He said, fiercely, "Good."

He nearly tripped when Stevie dragged them over a broken-limbed bush some bigger body had stumbled through. The forest melted a path for their feet where it had thrown obstacles for Floyd's. Though Leslie had lost all sense of their location, or the direction the man had fled, he trusted his boy's instincts.

"Trail's getting warmer," Stevie murmured.

The clamoring creek obscured the noise of their passage. Branches ghosted past and drooping leaves licked across Leslie's scalp wound, the trees tasting him. Shafts of moonlight fell through the canopy to caress the strong lines of his boy's outstretched arms nudging foliage aside. On some unseen signal, their pace began to slow.

"Nearly on him now," he breathed. "Let me lure him, say I need to parley, what with everything going down around town."

"Then what?" Leslie asked.

He turned on his heel, catching Leslie's resultant stumble and keeping him upright. His skin rippled and shifted from beneath. "Then, I kill him with my teeth. You can watch if you want. After that's done, when I'm satisfied, I'll go along wherever you say."

*You can watch* made the fine hairs on Leslie's body stand up. The boundaries between fear, compulsion, and desire were thin and clingy as sap. He thought about his bloodied feet; his split lip, busted nose, and lacerated hands; the reverberations of a murderous hymn buried in his cochlea . . . and nodded. Stevie grinned vicious in return. Leslie had seen and delivered death before, but he imagined the experience would be entirely different at the hands of this exquisite boy-creature with claws already peeking from his fingertips. Something bloody, hallowed by the forest's grace; an honest and natural communion.

Another few steps, and the clumsy tracks Floyd had left joined onto a disused path. Ahead through the trees the Spar glowed under heavy moonlight. Stevie reached a hand backward to pat Leslie's side, then said, "Stay on, here, and lend me those boots again." Without protest, Leslie crouched and unlaced them. His boy's attention was pointer-focused on the forest opposite their position, and the second he'd knotted the boots on again he darted off through the gloom.

By himself, Leslie found the conversations of nightbirds overhead and the pressure of the forest instantly eerier. How far ahead was Floyd, and what if he didn't fall for Stevie's ploy? What if, somehow, another member of the congregation found them first? Leslie's nerves doubled and tripled as dire scenarios cascaded through his mind's eye. But he'd been told to wait, so wait he would. Orders—being *in service*—made his patience and suffering simpler.

An interminable time later, though it was likely fewer than ten minutes, footsteps and conversation hit his straining ears. Leslie crawled under the nearest brush for cover. Pastel mineral stones glittered around him like knives. He palmed his reliable switchblade, which Stevie had retrieved for him after its loss during the baptismal ruckus. Oncoming danger drummed in his chest. Though Floyd wasn't his to revenge himself upon, if and when his assistance was needed, he would be prepared.

As the voices came closer, he made out Floyd Marshall dismissively saying, "I'm mighty sorry about Hiram, but I can't take back what happened to him."

*What happened to him,* like a natural disaster had pulped

Collins's intestines. Leslie curled his lip. Stevie emerged onto the far-side creek bank, eyes darting once toward his hiding spot and away; the stage had been set. Marshall, still lathered in the fear-sweat he'd been pumping out during his flight, burst from the trees and grabbed Stevie around the biceps—as if to stop him from continuing onward, though he'd halted on his own. Leslie wished he'd kept the Hansalls' rifle. Blond, milk-white men made easy pickings on a moonlit night. Stevie allowed Marshall to turn him away from the Spar. He stood with loose posture beneath the man's bulky shadow, arm dangling from his grip.

Marshall said, greasily indulgent, "But I'm sure glad I found you out here, before anything worse happened. It's good you're finally willing to listen to reason. Dug yourself a hole too deep to get free without my help, huh?"

"I wouldn't go that far, Floyd Marshall," Stevie said.

"Other than letting me get my way, how your momma and everyone else wants, what could you possibly do now? There's no one left in your corner, not after we ran off that bitch nurse." Ugly amusement colored his smile and coated the easy lie about what had happened with Leslie. "You can't duel a whole town. Unless you stick by me, there's only Preacher Holladay's mercies waiting for you, and I don't think you want to see what those are going to be."

Marshall crowded closer and Stevie held his ground, heels dug into the muck. His chin lifted in defiance. Marshall snorted and released his arm, only to run his palm forward—groping his chest, judging by the flex of Stevie's shoulders. Leslie bit the open wound inside his cheek for patience. Dense shadows around the pair began to compress and compound as some internal force drew a coating of darkness up over Stevie's ankles, then his calves and thighs, then his back.

"Go on and try me," he whispered.

Marshall mistook the tonal shift for fear and chuckled, wrapping his arms around Stevie's waist. The seams of Stevie's slacks strained and frayed. A liquid blackness pooled on the nape of his neck and between the joints of his unresisting hands. Marshall bent down, forcing a kiss onto him; the angle and motion suggested he'd stuffed his tongue into Stevie's mouth.

His immediate, agonized shriek—muffled and hideously *wet*—made Leslie grin.

Muscles across his neck and torso spasmed as he attempted to bow backward, though his head stayed pinioned in place. A bass snarl cut through the clearing, scraping over the survival instincts in Leslie's brain stem. Marshall beat frantic fists against Stevie's shoulders and head, his scream almost a pig-squeal. The boy laughed, muffled by the flesh trapped between his teeth, before he wrenched his head sideways. The sound of muscle tearing with a sucking-wet rip accompanied the motion.

Marshall reeled backward, freed from the embrace at last. His hands flapped at the blood pouring from his hollowed-out, gaping mouth. Bellows of agony echoed from earth to firmament. Staggering toward Stevie, the whites of his eyes flashing, he stumbled instead over a tree root and fell onto his face. The yowling never ceased. Gore splattered the dirt, almost black under the starlight.

Stevie spat the tongue out like a mouthful of chaw.

"You thought you were going to fuck me again?" Stevie asked. He unbuckled his belt and thumbed loose his trouser buttons while Marshall scrambled onto all fours. "That's real fucking funny, you arrogant piece of shit. I'm going to eat you raw."

Clouds blew past the moon and plunged them into darkness; discarded clothes landed on the ground by Leslie. Marshall pitched around toward the underbrush from whence he'd first come with the finesse of an ox. The sounds of his boy *becoming* filled the clearing, bones crunching into new positions and flesh splitting like shredding silk. Then came a second of quiet, punctured by a predator's growl. The clouds scuttled away again, revealing Marshall's bloody trail and the awesome creature whose muzzle-mouth lowered toward it. Leslie read the quirked thin lips and bladed teeth as smiling. The creature's haunches flexed, flinging its mass into the trees. Screams rang cacophonously through the night. Leslie rose from his hiding place to settle by the Spar again, sweating through an overwhelm close to spiritual ecstasy.

Crashing and sobbing announced Marshall before he burst onto the creek again a mere yard or so down the bank—easily herded in his disoriented, terrified state. Though he froze at the sight of another person, his split second of relief melted into horror when he realized who was looking back at him. The pause was more than long enough. Stevie, in all his sublime monstrosity, plowed into Marshall from behind.

Leslie stood on the sidelines with hands tucked in his pockets, appreciating the rush of the stream around his ankles. Marshall, flattened on his stomach beneath the creature's weight, flung his hand out and *wailed*—tongueless but pleading. Glowing, lantern-yellow eyes met Leslie's before it angled its gaze downward to its prey. Hooked talons forced between the gaps of Marshall's ribs right below his scapula: lungs, kidneys, liver within reach. He clawed for purchase on the earth but it refused him, sliding from under his fingernails. The creature bounced its weight down hard; its talons popped through bone and viscera, and Marshall's shrieking flattened on a gurgle. For another four or five seconds, a hideous retching sound escaped his body—and then he simply ceased.

The forest deity atop his corpse, however, carried on. Its

vengeful dismemberment was gruesome to watch, despite Leslie's own knowledge and experience. Still, he refused to turn away, though after another few minutes he had to sit down beside the creek again. The cold water coursing around his ankles kept his gorge from rising high enough to gag him. Ribbons of blood trickled from the scene on the banks, filtering into the stream—which merrily babbled onward toward town. After shredding the corpse into scattered meat, the creature finally sat back on its haunches. Ruptured guts fouled the breeze. Slow and thoughtful, the handsome thing bent its head, opened its mouth, and tore loose a bite from—Leslie slapped a hand over his eyes rather than confirm which *part* had been selected. He couldn't hear the chewing over the burble of the Spar, but he imagined it nonetheless.

Water splashing was his only warning before the creature knocked his arm down. It crouched over him, streaked with carnage and utterly alien in its beauty. Flesh scraps lingered between its teeth. One nimbly jointed paw pressed against his chest, gentle but implacable, until he collapsed onto his elbows. Careful claws snipped through the threads of his shirt buttons. Its rank breath puffed in his face.

"You cannot be serious," he whispered.

The creature tucked its muzzle beneath his ear, huffed his scent, and then rested its open maw around his throat as delicate as a lace collar. Leslie froze. Instinct held him still, though the teeth hadn't nicked him. This monster was his boy; his boy was this monster. Leslie gasped as it shredded his undershirt down the middle, baring his tits. An answering, eager groan vibrated its teeth around his neck. Tattered fabric clung around his armpits. The gripping jaws released, and he tilted his head to peer into its curious eyes as it measured his reactions in turn. Leslie allowed himself to *feel*: the pulse throbbing through his throat and guts, the pebbled nipples, the euphoria of survival, and the satisfaction of a job completed.

His own very real pleasure at seeing justice done.

Leslie gazed skyward as he unbuttoned his trousers. The creature leaned aside enough for him to wriggle them loose, soaked and clinging, and he thanked the hills that he didn't straight away plant his bare ass on a chunk of fluorspar.

"Get in the water," he grumbled.

The creature scooped an arm around his waist and effortlessly dragged them toward the center of the stream. Scant hours before, he'd been baptized beneath this same creek in hatred and terror—but now it embraced them tenderly, sluiced blood and dirt from their bodies. "All right, then," he said, bolstering his courage, and splayed his legs wide.

The creature dropped onto all fours and, almost purring, plunged its long tongue right into his mouth. He gagged, both from the meat stuck between its teeth and the intense pressure on his soft palate. One paw clutched the top of his skull while the other scraped burning lines across his thigh. Its head shifted, strange flat nose pressed to his cheek; the angle allowed its tongue to penetrate the clutching squeeze of his throat. Leslie smacked at its shoulders, then grabbed it around the solid-muscled waist. The flesh beneath his hands was rough, porous like the coal seams it had been drawn from—until all at once it smoothed, became silken as night air made flesh, sliding easily over the hard muscle beneath. Embracing the impossible, astounding thing was like trying to hold a whole mountain in his arms.

The smothering kiss ended as the creature withdrew its tongue and left Leslie gasping, covered in copper-smelling drool from nose to chin. Its mineral-rock teeth found the thickest part of his deltoid and dug down with just enough pressure to puncture. The fiery streak of pain-pleasure made him yelp; his cunt clenched. The paw beneath his thigh lifted and pushed, contorting him until his lower body was held suspended. He felt as if he'd balled into an entirely new shape, and though he assumed he knew what came next, he hadn't been fucked in so long he barely remembered how. Another throb of desire washed through him, enhanced by mild sweet fear, as he considered its claws and teeth, his vulnerable soft skin, and the dismembered corpse less than twelve feet from their consummation.

Something firm, rounded, and thick pressed against the cleft of his ass.

He shoved at the creature's torso, and when it obligingly angled backward what he saw between its legs gave the impression of a cock: a blunt, ready instrument, similar to the strap he'd left behind in Chicago. Uneasy need coiled below his belly. Leslie was less surprised the shapeshifting entity had produced a dick and more by the size it had chosen. While he gawped, the thing changed again, growing a sinuous curve.

"Oh, fuck," he whispered.

Its tip bumped against his clit. Their lengths glided, easy and slick, against one another. The friction alone drew an airy moan from his throat. Seeing the measure of its cock laid along his stomach made his thighs flex. His fist closed around its shaft, gave one firm tug, and then guided the head into place against his cunt. He'd thought himself prepared, but when it forced through the clenched resistance of his unused hole he *shouted.* The bullying stretch burned, and it immediately plunged deep, bruising at the end of his capacity. He hadn't ever been fucked like this, certainly not during the light fumbles he'd accepted on the front.

His boy-monster huffed and growled, its hold shifting around to the front of his thighs—trapping his legs together and aloft while it pummeled away at his guts. Water splashed and sloshed around them, intensifying the sting of each impact between its haunches and his backside. The short thrusts knocked loose grunts loud enough to be screams. Helpless to silence himself and desperate for an orgasm, Leslie stuffed a clumsy hand between his thighs. One swift, mean pinch at his clit made him spasm tighter around the creature's dick; the abrupt increase in pressure, pain, and pleasure hurled him over the edge by surprise. Losing his core tension and his precarious balance as he came, Leslie collapsed backward under the creek surface. Cool water poured into his ears, nose, and mouth, such that he felt, for a moment, overfilled in every possible space.

Before the shock registered, the remnants of climax still firing through his nerves, the creature hoisted him out of the creek entirely. An iron bar of an arm supported his back, and the other clutched his legs against its torso, their groins nestled together with it buried to the hilt. Somehow, even motionless, the dick continued to bulge and swell. Pressed against every oversensitized inch of his insides, the growing width felt as if it might split him in two. Leslie wheezed, limp and overwrought, weightless in its grasp. The creature watched his face: hungry, devout. *One blood and one flesh,* he thought deliriously, *isn't that what a marriage is?* Its paw curled over his shoulder. Claws pricked the wing of his collarbone. With only the strength in its arms and haunches, as if he were lighter than a rag doll, the creature dragged his body back and forth along its length until a second climax rocked through him. He'd never come just from being fucked before and the surprise had him sobbing for air. The dampness on his face was either tears or saliva. White lights flared behind his eyelids.

"Stop, stop," he slurred.

His monster halted immediately, teeth glistening and eyes afire.

Leslie smacked at the arm around his legs with a nerveless hand. The made-to-measure cock shrank mercifully quick, though it remained inside him as he flexed his cramping toes. Spending so long submerged in the creek had him shivering despite the heat of being loved brainless. Overhead the moon had traveled nearer the bowl of the hills.

"We need to go," he gasped.

The actual withdrawal hurt. After his preternatural partner settled on its haunches again, Leslie probed himself for injury—delicately thrilled by the unfamiliar *loose* sensation. Such literal openness had been forbidden to him by role and expectation, but as proof that he'd been well-handled, he found he enjoyed it. The creature's animate shadows, like ash runoff, melted into the suction of the creek and its surrounding gory mud. Stevie emerged triumphant, his freckled, tanned body damply glistening. He took Leslie's free hand and lifted him from the creek with ease. Standing upright felt strange, downright bow-legged.

"How has nobody showed up, with all that screaming?" he asked.

An observant owl hooted at their noise.

"They're cowards," Stevie said. He handed Leslie's trousers over and asked, sly, "Was I good? I could do it longer next time, long as you can handle."

"Jesus, I couldn't take any more." Stevie oozed boyish smugness. Leslie's bitten shoulder stung, and he craned his neck to inspect the wound, saying, "That's going to scar."

"Good," Stevie replied. "You think I fucked you too hard to run?"

Leslie glowered, blushing despite himself. "I'll be paying you back for this, you know."

"Looking forward to it, sir," he said. "But for now, if the townsfolk are still occupied with their preacher man's night sermon, I know where to steal a horse."

Leslie threw his clothes at him, heart kicking at the possibility of getting the hell out of town. The clearing had begun to crawl with scavenger bugs drawn to the stench of the dead man's remains—or, at least, the parts that hadn't been eaten. Leslie ran his tongue over his teeth to chase away the lingering taste. His first baptism had been a violation, but the second was a renewal.

# XV.

Stevie prowled barefoot over and through tangling hunter's trails that Leslie had never so much as noticed before, guiding their roundabout return to Spar Creek. The night's travails had begun to ache in his strained muscles, his bumps and scratches and bruises.

Over his shoulder, Stevie said, "The church ain't far off now."

Having no sense of their whereabouts, Leslie grunted understanding.

"It's funny, how those men all tried to keep us locked up in town, saying the hills were satanic," Stevie continued, breathing effortlessly as if he were strolling along a promenade. "Seems to me that what's here is only right and natural. God knows it feels good to be so strong, and powerful, and *alive*. Must be just that, what they're so damn scared of: people getting free of them."

"Always is," he said.

A golden square of light floated on the horizon, past the tree line. Their conversation clipped short. The forest terminated around the backside of the parsonage house, which lay coldly dark—but the meetinghouse windows farther in the distance cast arrogant noise and light onto the night beyond. With silent, stalking tread the pair crept close enough for a vantage on the people inside.

Though the late gathering numbered fewer than regular Sunday sermon, it was far larger than Leslie had anticipated, and also more full of familiar faces. With a betrayed disappointment he spotted kindly Jackson Hansall. The unobstructed sight lines onto their milling, fragile bodies—assumed safe within their sanctuary while his boy, monstrous hungers leashed for the time being, crouched observantly outside—gave Leslie a nauseous thrill.

"I saw a demon tonight," Ames Holladay shouted, pacing the length of the pulpit. His ruddy face and swinging arms telegraphed desperation. "A devil black as Hell. The demon came for the nurse, foul woman, that Jezebel who brought sin among us."

Caught by the sermon and wondering how long the preacher had already been hollering at his congregants, Leslie didn't expect the palm that chafed over his sore crotch through his trousers.

"Sin, huh?" Stevie muttered, sweetly nasty.

Leslie flicked his knuckles, hissing *hush*.

Within the sanctuary, Holladay carried on. "I propose drastic measures this night: firstly we find that woman, and if she still lives, expel her from our midst. Secondly, we resolve the matter of Brother Marshall's claim on Stephanie Mattingly, and bring her to heel in her appropriate role."

The crowd murmured solid agreement. Stevie pressed his smiling mouth against Leslie's ear and murmured, "Has anyone started to worry where he's wandered off to, you think?"

"Let's go," Leslie whispered, but received a shake of the head in reply.

Stevie hissed, "I wanna hear what he says."

"—and Brother Marshall has repented for his transgression," Holladay continued. "He was tempted, and he succumbed, but he has promised to make his trespass legitimate by the law, and by the Lord. I will join them, beneath the eyes of God, and mend the breach with the holy bonds of matrimony."

"Amen, Father," said a woman from the front pew.

"Before the marriage, however, I will exorcise her—for as many days and nights as it takes to drive the satan out—so that they may be joined in renewed purity," Holladay finished.

"He'd have to kill me," Stevie said.

The rumble of consensus among the congregation showed who the townsfolk really were, at the end of the line. There was no hemming or hawing, no signs of discontent. All the proper, modest girls and boys who'd been raised alongside Stevie stayed silent, as did Jackson Hansall and his glowering wife and everyone else. Whatever secret misgivings they might hold in their hearts, their heads and hands pledged cruelty.

"At the sunrise, then, we'll go and find her out," said Holladay. "Now, let us pray."

The pastor bowed his head over his clasped hands.

Stevie tugged Leslie's shirt collar and drew him back across the parsonage lawn into the woods. Once protected by the trees, he said, "Those fuckers should keep praying 'til dawn. Now come along, this way—Old Moss boards his mare at the tobacco barn. We'll take her, and do something else for this damned town besides."

On the backside of the town's shared tobacco barn, Stevie wiggled a false board loose to retrieve the spare key beneath. The pitch darkness between the building and the surrounding hills was so impenetrable that Leslie had to hold on for guidance again. He couldn't see an inch ahead of his face, but his ears worked overtime, so he heard the padlock tumblers clunk. Stevie grasped his hands and placed them onto a wooden grip. Together they pried the sliding door open wide enough to creep inside. Their scents and sounds provoked a nervous whinny from the horse they'd come to steal.

"Where are the extra work clothes?" Leslie murmured.

Stevie released his hands and left him floating in unbounded nothingness. The noise of his rustling around, clucking soothingly at the horse and striking a match, filled the darkness. Thankfully, the match kindled his lantern on the first try. Stevie hung the lamp from a center post, its shadows leaping onto a ceiling furred with tobacco leaves, and pointed Leslie to a large cabinet. While he saddled the grumpy mare, Leslie grabbed a musty shirt and trousers from the stored spares.

He'd barely thumbed the last button on his stolen shirt closed when Ames Holladay barked, "Stop where you stand."

Leslie spooked as hard as the horse. Stevie cussed, grabbing for the mare as she bustled backward, tossing her head loose from the bridle. Her panicked whinnying was terribly loud. Stevie clucked and hushed; Leslie turned to face their troubles.

Holladay stood alone in the doorway. The electric lantern he clutched overhead cast the peaks and valleys of his face in demoniac relief. He strode into the barn confidently, his glare sweeping over each of them in turn, but . . . Leslie glanced over his shoulder. No congregant posse waited at his back, as though he'd left them patiently awaiting his return at the sermon house, sure of his handle on the situation. Sure, it seemed, that he'd capture these willful creatures himself.

Leslie slipped his switchblade into his palm.

"I saw you," Holladay said, meanly soft. "As soon as I lifted my head from prayer, the good Lord showed you to me, sneaking off from my church. I knew you'd run, rather than face the consequences of your sins."

Refractive yellow splashed across Stevie's eyes—but the mare jolted from his soothing hands the second he began to change, panicked again, and on the next blink his pupils were normal. Leslie shook his head and released the frustrated groan that had been nesting in his lungs since the night he rode into Spar Creek.

Holladay lifted a hand. In his most paternalistic tone, he said, "I am generous enough to allow your departure, Miss Bruin, but you cannot take Miss Mattingly along."

One measured step in front of another, Leslie approached the pastor. His smile professed self-indulgence, as if he expected acquiescence or apology—or, maybe, a plea for mercy he could deny. Leslie had sat back as witness for one act of vengeance; in doing so, he felt he'd earned his own as well.

"You're beaten, Miss—"

Within striking distance, Leslie whipped the switchblade from his pocket and triggered its release. The rattlesnake speed spooked Holladay into raising his forearms—but Leslie was already in motion. He angled the knife skyward and jammed the entire length through the bullseye of the pastor's Adam's apple. Bodyweight momentum buried the blade to its hilt.

Holladay's icy blue eyes held no comprehension. An inhuman croak vibrated the knife, which had lodged clean through the throat and chin, trapping his loud mouth shut. The pastor planted both hands on Leslie's shoulders in a parody of benediction. Arterial spray splattered his face. Leslie released his grip and shoved Holladay over. The pastor collapsed onto his side, convulsively scrabbling at the handle protruding from his neck. The mare protested the carnage smell with another cry, though Stevie tried to shush her, tunelessly whistling.

"Take her on out," Leslie said.

"Yessir," Stevie answered.

Prancing, nervous hooves clopped away as Leslie stood over Ames Holladay. His final bodily release smelled foul, but there was satisfaction in watching his heels cease their dragging. Once he stilled, an atmospheric shift passed through the vaulted barn, the familiar whisper of something from the other side—before Leslie crouched to unlace his good boots. With socks stuffed into the toes, they'd fit all right. Lastly, he used his old shirt to grip the switchblade's slippery handle and pry it free. The blade had notched on some bone or another; he'd need to get it serviced later.

Outside, carrying the pastor's stolen electric lantern, he found Stevie hauling a canister of gasoline from the barn's generator. The realization struck him once Stevie began to pour the pungent accelerant around the baseboards of the building, which held the year's entire tobacco crop, the core of the town's finances and continued survival.

"Giving them one last hurrah, are you?" he murmured.

Stevie lifted his head. Several emotions crossed his face, unreadable for the most part, but Leslie thought he understood anyway. How they'd turned on him, betrayed him in his hour of need: he'd give the same right back.

"It's what they deserve," he said.

Leslie levered onto the horse's back, waiting one last time as Stevie struck every match in his pocketbook onto the gasoline, the hay, the wood boards, anything that might catch. As the flames caught and spread, their hungry glow flickered across the pastor's corpse, and that was the closest thing to hellfire Leslie had ever believed in.

Stevie boosted himself onto the saddle ahead of Leslie. They rode unseen from the holler with the scent of burning tobacco following them on the night breeze. Leslie tucked his nose against Stevie's neck, their mare cautiously picking her footing through the woods, and heaved a breath. Sweat musk eased the pressure in his sinuses—tingling from the smoke, certainly, but also from *feeling* stronger than he understood how to handle.

# EPILOGUE

Two handsome men—or, something like it—sat together sipping ice-cream floats at the Sears, Roebuck and Company soda fountain on the corner of 8th and Broadway. Their waitress, a middle-aged woman whose nametag read "Lilly," checked on them three times as often as they'd have preferred. The train for Chicago wasn't due to depart until evening, so Les figured he'd show his companion the sights to pass time. The worry that a policeman would come haul them off for questioning about the death of some boonies pastor had finally begun to disperse. Maybe the people of Spar Creek had decided to handle their own mess, and leave everyone else out of it. Good riddance, as far as Les was concerned.

Whenever he got nervy, though, the best treatment was stealing a peek at the starry-eyed way Stevie consumed the world around him. He tried to play it cool when he noticed someone watching, but the ice-cream float had knocked even that feigned maturity loose. The boy was grinning ear to ear, licking the neck of the spoon clean once the drink was gone. The pink curl of his tongue furrowed around and slid up the silver strut. Les cleared his throat.

"Can I get y'all anything more?" asked Lilly.

"I think we're through, miss," Les said.

"Shame to see such good-looking fellas go," she sighed, touching her knuckles to her chest. "Even if I'm old enough to be your mother!"

"You don't look a day over thirty," he replied with a wink. Stevie stamped his foot on the rail below the counter. The waitress laughed, turning away for their check, and Les leaned over to mutter, "Didn't I already say we're going steady, boy?"

"You're a lech," he whispered back.

For the sake of travel and a low profile, Les had bound his chest and shaved his head high and tight. Stevie himself had been done over into a proper young gentleman with his dark hair cropped short around the ears, emphasizing his strong jawline. Plus, his chest seemed to flatten another centimeter every time he shifted between forms. The happy glitter in his eyes lent him a mischievous air, and the suit Les had paid for, once they'd reached a city where he could access his bank account, did him several more favors. There was something richly pleasurable about passing through places as a man, entirely unremarked upon, though the experience rested differently on his shoulders than Stevie's.

Leslie paid their tab and hooked their elbows together to draw them onto the street once more. The nearest clock read 2:15. They had until almost six to dawdle.

"Would you like to see the Brown Hotel? It's famous, and it's got a bookshop on the first floor," Les offered.

"*You* might like the bookshop," Stevie said. "Didn't I tell you?"

"Tell me what?" he asked, navigating through pedestrian traffic.

Stevie huffed. "I can't much read, at least not good."

His *can't* sounded more like *cain't,* plaintive and mildly embarrassed. Les glanced up at his face, shrugged, and said, "No reason I can't show you how, is there?"

"Think of something I can do in return, and it's a deal," he said.

"Fine, fine. When we get to Chicago, we'll get you some papers. Have you thought if you want another name?" he asked.

Stevie stayed silent for several minutes.

"Stephen," he said. Les fought a smile, making a note to read to him from Radclyffe Hall's novel about his possible namesake sometime. "But, say: How do you like your last name?"

The boy sounded nervous. Bubbles of delight and anxiety fizzed in Les's chest. He'd never come close to doing this sort of thing before, not in his entire life. Tentatively, he said, "Once when a friend of mine decided to get a house, she adopted her girl through the courts. For the inheritance."

Stevie laughed. "Maybe later, if you're that keen on being my old man. Why don't we just start with names?"

Les squeezed his forearm, fond. As they strolled the waterfront metro the bones of Clark Memorial Bridge rose into sight. Steel girders mapped a thoroughly modern passage from their side of the river straight across to the other, signaling an oncoming future the likes of which Les couldn't entirely picture. The department store's glass facade reflected gold sunlight down on their heads. Northward, across the meandering Ohio River, was another city—another life. Stevie bumped shoulders with him, and together, they waited for the streetlight to change.

# ACKNOWLEDGMENTS

As usual, first I've got to dedicate my gratitude and affection to the people who give me their support, patience, and love daily. For the friends and chosen family without whom I couldn't get through the days—Brett, Dave, Emrys, Emilie, Trisha, and my mother, among so many others—thank you always. Without your careful tending, I'd simply shrivel and perish.

For the group chats and writers' circles and internet pals: it's because of you that I've kept my grip on sanity over the last few years. Without your friendship and conversation, without our shared places for being horny, weird, nasty, thoughtful, incisive, and sometimes catty . . . I honestly don't know what I'd do. Thanks also for providing a communal zone where I can yowl and gnash my teeth over queer media, various hot celebrity dudes who kiss each other on the mouth, my boundless love for BTS, et cetera.

And speaking of queer media, *The Woods All Black* definitely owes something to how creatively charged and replenished I felt after watching the mature, intense, sexy feast that was *KinnPorsche: La Forte* . . . then rewatching *Hannibal*. I can't say thank you enough to those shows (and many others!) for once again reminding me, "Oh shit—*that's* what gay art can do!" Thanks also to RM's new album *Indigo,* which spoke to me in a moment when I was really struggling with my craft and the ideas I had about making art long term.

Big thanks as well to my agents past and present, Tara Gilbert and Kate McKean, and to the Tordotcom team for your tireless work and support. I'm especially grateful to my editor, Carl Engle-Laird, who was *very* patient with me when writing this novella took three times longer than I'd initially planned. Additional thanks to Matt Rusin, Christine Foltzer, Libby Collins, Samantha Friedlander, Lauren Hougen, Dakota Griffin, Steven Bucsok, Christina MacDonald, Melanie Sanders, and Winn Foreman. One final thanks to the archives at the University of Kentucky and their collection of primary source materials—including recorded interviews with some of the actual nurses who served in the FNS from its founding.

Lastly, I thought readers might appreciate some references for further reading—bonus content! On the one hand, I drew stylistic inspiration from a wealth of novels and poems (many of which were by queer writers, or about queer life) published through the late '20s and early '30s. Those include but aren't limited to . . .

*In Search of Lost Time* by Marcel Proust (1922–1931, English translations)
*The Waste Land* by T. S. Eliot (1922)
*Cane* by Jean Toomer (1923)
*Mrs. Dalloway* by Virginia Woolf (1925)
*The Weary Blues* by Langston Hughes (1926)
*The Sun Also Rises* by Ernest Hemingway (1926)
*The Well of Loneliness* by Radclyffe Hall (1928)
*Home to Harlem* by Claude McKay (1928)
*Decline and Fall* by Evelyn Waugh (1928)
*Orlando: A Biography* by Virginia Woolf (1928)

*Passing* by Nella Larson (1929)
*A Room of One's Own* by Virginia Woolf (1929)
*Christopher and His Kind: A Memoir, 1929–1939* by Christopher Isherwood (1976)

On the other hand, it's obviously a historical novella, so I had to gather mountains of research on everything from the Frontier Nursing Service itself; to queer life, language, and politics in the interwar period; to the heavily racialized and eugenic nature of medicine, reproductive justice, and philanthropy at the time. With that in mind, here's some further reading to get you started . . .

Bronski, Michael. *A Queer History of the United States*. Beacon Press, 2011.
Faderman, Lillian. *Odd Girls and Twilight Lovers: A History of Lesbian Life in Twentieth-Century America*. Columbia University Press, 1991.
*The Forgotten Frontier* [Silent Film]. Frontier Nursing Service, Inc., 1931.
Goan, Melanie. *Mary Breckinridge: The Frontier Nursing Service and Rural Health in Appalachia*. UNC Press, 2008.
Lewis, Anne. *Frontier Nursing Service*. Documentary Film. Appalshop, Inc., 1984.
Miller, Ben and Huw Lemmey. *Bad Gays: A Homosexual History*. Verso Press, 2022.
Newman, Louise. *White Women's Rights: The Racial Origins of Feminism in the United States*. Oxford University Press, 1999.
Rupp, Leila J. *Sapphistries: A Global History of Love between Women*. NYU Press, 2009.

Sedgwick, Eve Kosofvsky. *Epistemology of the Closet.* University of California Press, 1990.

Snorton, C. Riley. *Black on Both Sides: Racial History of Trans Identity.* University of Minnesota Press, 2017.

Somerville, Siobhan B. *Queering the Color Line: Race and the Invention of Homosexuality in American Culture.* Duke University Press, 2000.

Stryker, Susan. *Transgender History: The Roots of Today's Revolution.* 2nd ed. Seal Press, 2017.

Washington, Harriet A. *Medical Apartheid: The Dark History of Medical Experimentation on Black Americans from Colonial Times to the Present.* Anchor Press, 2008 (Reprint).

Zarrelli, Natalie. "In the Early 20th Century, America Was Awash in Incredible Queer Nightlife." *Atlas Obscura.* April 14, 2016.

In closing, endless gratitude to everyone who bought this book, or requested it from their library, or loaned their copy to a friend. You keep my lights on, a roof over my head, and food on my table. It's your continued support that allows me to craft these strange gay stories.

Thank you.